~Things Come Apart~

A novel by

Kijana Scott-Jackson, Ph.D.

Dedicated to my three reasons ...

Nia

Lauryn

Jeremy

This work is developed from a real-life person, people, or events, but with many differences.

~ Intro ~

One: **Foundation**

~the basis or groundwork of anything~

-1-

Man, where do I begin? This is a sordid, twisted, and complicated story. It tells a tale of love, lust, lies, and lessons. The main character in this story is named Lena Joi Timmons. She is a Chicago native; born and bred. She is a girl's girl; always has been. She likes looking and feeling "put together" at all times. She is fierce. She is intelligent. She is accomplished. She is always there for others. She is broken inside. She does an amazing job hiding it; until she no longer can. She is … "me." I am all those things. I am Lena. My general philosophy is appearances set the tone, at least that's what I'd always been taught. Pretty on the outside, with beauty exuding from the inside. I've had some amazing role models in my life, so I am honored and privileged to carry it on. Kind, sweet, lovely Lena; that's what people see and experience with me. That's what people say about me. Even when I don't see it or feel it in myself. I work hard to please people, always seeking to accommodate or help in some way, sometimes to a fault. But don't let the sweet demeanor fool you, I *can* go from zero to 100 quick. Quick, quick; also, sometimes to a fault. This isn't what I'd view as a redeeming quality. It's something I've worked hard to control, even suppress at times. Because when I'm "*gone or in the zone*," I'm literally in another stratosphere and it can be hard to bring myself out of that dark place. I have found myself so wound up in anger that it's almost crippling. It's taken me to reach my adult years to begin to peel away the layers that help to explain where the anger and darkness come from. I'm still a work in progress. All praise to the "*highest*" for the gift of therapy! It has truly been my saving grace.

Now, one thing about me that needs no therapeutic intervention is knowing and proudly proclaiming that I am a Chicago native tried and true. In fact, I love everything about Chicago. The sights, the smells, the food, the lakefront, the radio stations, the nightlife, and most of all downtown Chicago. There is just nothing and no place like "the Chi." I tried to leave home a few times, went to the East Coast (DC, Virginia, Maryland), and then the Southern states (Alabama, Georgia, Tennessee), but something always called me back. I hear people complain about the cold in Chicago and unpredictable weather patterns, but I enjoy the experience of having four seasons. You can bask in the transitions of the weather and honestly, the anticipation of those transitions is what makes it all worthwhile. There is nothing like summertime in Chicago. Riding in a car along the full stretch of Lake Shore Drive listening to music, vibing to the nighttime energy, marveling at the beaches and people watching…it just doesn't get any better!

I am a Child and Adolescent Psychiatrist by trade, I have a Master's in Adolescent Psychology, I am a certified Licensed Clinical Mental Health Professional, I have a PsyD. in Clinical Behavioral Psychology and I hold a Ph.D. in Counseling. It's a lot, I know. I knew early on that I wanted to work with youth with a specialty focus on behavior and mental health, primarily in the African American community.

It simply intrigued me, and I love everything about the field. It is, however, extremely exhausting and most times takes a toll on my sense of self and my mental health. I have seen the toll of not having access to mental health professionals and mental health programs has had on our community and I wanted to affect change in this area. I remember my experiences in high school with friends or associates who were struggling in one way or another with mental health issues, which were often undiagnosed or misunderstood. They were afraid to say something about their feelings because they worried about being labeled or falling into the stigma that black folks hold on to related to mental health. In the black family, it is not uncommon to see or experience someone in your family displaying odd behaviors. And then the aunties and grandmas say things like, "*Chile you know he slow", "Aw yeah, Junebug special"*. Then come up with these old, hokey, down-home remedies to correct the behaviors. Drink this. Eat that. Put this here. Stand in the corner. Blah. Blah. Blah. I hate that. I wanted to get rid of that stigma and show our black and brown families that it's *ok to not be ok.* And to educate them on how to begin to approach it from a different lens. Shit, I'm an adult and strive hard to remind myself of that every damn day based on my challenges. I carry a heavy, heavy load. I am also the "wearer" of many hats; too many damn hats if I'm being honest. Yet here I am in my mid-forties, with all these degrees and life experiences feeling like everything before today has been a fucking blur. Life has happened and it has happened hard. Childhood shit, adolescent shit, teen to early adulthood shit. Lots of SHIT! Not in the way that one may surmise from that last statement, perhaps I'm being a bit dramatic. That's also me; I'm also known for being dramatic as hell. I stand in it and own it. Hello, my name is Lena Timmons and I'm a fucking drama queen! It is what it is. My *Ganna* (grandma) used to say '*Tell the truth and shame the devil'*… so here goes. I'll tell you my truth. This is my story.

I am the daughter of Raymond Lee Timmons and Marvea Olivia Weston-Timmons. Raymond (or Ray) is a handsome, charismatic, highly intelligent, low-key narcissist. I mean, above all things, he loves himself immensely which isn't a bad thing necessarily, but he is completely devoid of empathy. Dada is a lifelong businessman. He's been in the investment game for as long as I can remember and has made quite a comfortable life for himself and his family. Dada always kept the news channels on in our house when we were growing up. Listen, half of what they said on the shows he watched confused me and the other half of what Dada said confirmed that I wasn't interested in Finance and Business, at all. That was definitely his thing. As I got older, channels like CNN Money, Fox Business, Financial Times, and CNBC were kept on the TV and in heavy rotation. Dada wanted to see anything, everything that gave him financial updates, the latest stock prices, and activity on the Dow Jones index. BORING!!!! Talk to me about a good bottle of wine a fancy dinner at a fancy restaurant, or the latest research on anything related to Child and Adolescent development and I'm all in. That other stuff, not so much.

Dada also loves the finer things; the best homes, the best restaurants, the best resorts, the best cars, big boats, fast motorcycles, you know all the big boy toys and all things flashy and shiny. Finance is his career, but his top-tier and most important role is being a father. He loves his children, without question. He would do anything for us. There are just the two of us, and I am the only girl. Because of that, I sometimes feel like Dada pushed me harder intentionally to ensure I'd be able to hold my own. He is the one who taught me the importance of taking up space in the room. He'd say, "*Don't let anyone tell you what or who you can be,*" "*Walk in every room and be bold, be proud, be unapologetically you.*" I think he knew that being a black woman in any field or industry would present challenges for me that would be different than the ones my brother would face. Not that he wouldn't also be challenged, but it would be different. I trusted Dada's guidance and used to hang on to every word he spoke. Nothing he said to me ever felt wrong and in my opinion, everything about Dada was just right; until it wasn't, but I'll get to that later. He was a hard worker; a strong provider and he taught me the value of what hard work could offer. He took pride in making sure we lived in a beautiful home, in a safe neighborhood, with the very best schools to attend. He drove the nicest cars and was simply pulled together. Dada was always sharp! He was a man's man and exuded a confidence that no one could deny. What many didn't know, however, is his upbringing was extremely humble and he wasn't as sure of himself as a child. He was a very shy kid and often bullied. He'd share stories from his childhood with me and my brother and I believe it's those experiences that framed him into the man he ultimately became. Big. Bold. Not taking any shit. But there was also a side to him that could be cold, selfish, and mean; even towards the ones who were closest to and loved him most. Growing up I loved everything about Dada; he was a superhero in my eyes. The epitome and model of the man I would eventually aim to seek out as a partner in my adult years. The looks, charisma, intelligence, and go-getter approach to life, in my eyes, were the qualities I gravitated toward. This is the type of man I wanted to be my "forever" love. Dada's qualities shone brighter than the brightest star in the sky. Or so I thought. I'd later learn the hard way that everything that looks good to you ain't always good for you. In fact, in some instances, good was nowhere to be found and that bright, shiny shit easily tarnishes. And in the end, all you end up with is pain and disappointment.

Dada was the third child of five children. He had two older brothers and two younger sisters. One of his sisters died before she was 1 year old from a high fever. Dada often tells me that I looked just like her when I was a baby. His parents met when they were in their early teens and fell in love instantly. My "Poppy" Joseph was from Savannah, Georgia, and spent most of his working years as a laborer. He only had a 6th grade education so finding work was based on going out every day and essentially contracting himself out to do whatever work was available. That could include anything from landscaping, plumbing, electrical work, or delivering food items from the local grocery. Poppy was a "jack of all trades." He could do it all. He was also the most mild-mannered man I'd ever known. Always kind, always smiling, and very soft-spoken. But he knew the importance of hard work and believed in saving every penny he earned. He wasn't flashy or boastful at all, so it's weird to me that Dada is the exact opposite.

My "Ganna" Christiane was simply a jewel. She was a ball of warmth, softness, and love. I miss her so much; she passed away when I was in my early 20s. Ganna was from the Cayman Islands and spoke with a strong Caribbean accent. She had the smoothest skin and long black flowing hair. Her skin was the color of butterscotch and she always smelled good. Ganna and Poppy met when they were in their late teens. Ganna's family migrated to Savannah for better opportunities since it was known to be a cultural and historical hub of the South and was conveniently located near the Atlantic Ocean. Ganna came from a close, tight-knit family and she did not play when it came to taking care of her own family. She always stood by Poppy's side and took excellent care of their home. She was an amazing cook and always had a hot meal ready and waiting for Poppy when he came home every night. She never missed a morning without giving him a cup of hot coffee, one fried egg, and two pieces of bacon. It was like clockwork, each morning through rain, shine, sickness, etc. She would rarely allow us in her kitchen, cooking for her family, in her mind, was her "role." I personally believe it was her escape. Not in the sense of wanting to get away from us but more so to have something solely be *her thing* that she had complete control over. Ganna loved equally and unwaveringly hard on each one of her children and eventually became completely obsessed with her grandchildren. She doted on us. As the years progressed, I learned that she and my Dada had a strange dynamic. There was an unspoken tension between them every time they were around each other. It was clear that something was fractured there, but I wouldn't fully come to know what it was until much later in my life.

Now, my mother Marvea Olivia Weston-Timmons, or Mo, as she is affectionately known, is a diva personified. To put it plainly, she is all things "classy". Momma had worked for many years as a Real Estate broker and established an impeccable reputation. She was the "*face on the billboard*" type of broker. Everyone who was anyone in Chicago knew Mo Weston-Timmons. She was highly sought after, which came as no surprise because she was the total package! I would watch the way she paid close attention to everything and everyone that she encountered in her day-to-day movement. She had a way of ensuring everything was buttoned up, precise, and always in place. As a mother, she was fully invested in her children in the same way. We never wanted for or wondered about her love for us. It was as real as the sun setting in the West and the stars shining in the night sky. It was warm and soft like the thickest blanket on a cold winter's day. It was absolute. She took care of us, her home, and her husband with a level of care that you don't see much anymore. I tried to mimic, in my adult life, the ways of Momma but I always fell short. She'd made it look so easy, but I was never anywhere near being like Momma, not in any way. I fell short. Often.

Momma's childhood was "complex", to put it gently. She had a tumultuous relationship with her father who was often away from the house and her mother worked hard but was ill for most of her life. In fact, she passed away when Momma was in her early twenties. Momma was the eldest of 3 children and because her mother was often too sick to care for her kids, Momma had to step in. So much pressure for a young girl to manage but she did it without any missteps or complaints. She had a level of patience that was unmatched. That patience would carry through her young adult journey and ultimately to her life with Dada. In the beginning of their relationship, they would paint the town red, hanging out with friends. Momma and Dada loved to dance and go to any place that had live music. Growing up, I remember listening to their stories about partying until the wee hours of the morning and there was always music playing in our house. I knew the lyrics to so many old songs as a young child that my friends would look at me strangely. "*Girl, how do you know this music*?" they'd ask. But to me it was normal. I loved Marvin Gaye, Nancy Wilson, The O'Jays, The Temptations, Stevie Wonder, but my favorite group was Earth, Wind and Fire. It was all just damn good music! It's memories like these that would make me reflect on happier times in my home as a child. And there were many, without question. But there were tougher, not so happy times as well. Oh sorry, let's get back to Momma.

So, like I said Momma had the patience of a saint. I sometimes didn't know if she was going to explode in some "*calm before the storm*" scenario given all that she had to endure at times. My little brother and I knew how to push the envelope for sure, but Momma would hold steady and bring it all back together without breaking a sweat. She'd exercise the same level of patience (or what I'd call unbelievable restraint) when it came to Dada too. Lord knows he'd push every damn button and pull every lever there was. You see, Dada was fully aware of how handsome he was, as were a lot of people. Female people. Lots of them. Ridiculous amounts of them. This became a major problem in our household. Consistently and continually. I recall once in my teenage years, after one of his "*hiccups*," (this is the word I would associate to his cheating episodes), hearing him plead to Momma for forgiveness. "*Baby, I'm sorry. I fucked up. I'll never do it again. I need you baby. You mean the world to me. I made another mistake.*" I'd find myself waiting anxiously to hear something break or crash against the wall or even hear Momma cuss his ass out, but I never heard a peep. There was always only Dada's pleading words and then there was silence. Every single time. I could never understand it. I would be in my room saying all the things I'd wished Momma would. "*You lying motherfucker. It's over. You don't deserve me. I don't deserve this. I deserve better. You aren't shit.*" Instead would go on and on to myself letting him have it on Momma's behalf. Every time they'd go through it, I'd go off! I'd say it in a whisper, and then I'd scream it aloud in my head or into my pillow. And every time, tears followed. I'd even try to *will* her to say something. But she never did. Never. That broke my heart, for her. I loved my Dada, without question, but sometimes I hated his ways; especially when it came to Momma.

From the outside looking in my parents seemed like a copy/paste version of the fictional characters, Cliff, and Claire Huxtable from the Cosby Show. Hard working, educated, well established black folks with seemingly polite and well-behaved children, living in suburbia. They looked amazing together and apart; equally. They were always on point, on time, and on *it*. Period. This was the outward perception and the role they played, and it was well received. Believable. Admired. Perhaps even envied. But it was the stuff that happened when the doors closed that would affect *me* for life.

Dada was good at many things, honestly, he was good at most things. Solid in business, a master at public relations, good family man however, one thing he was not good at was managing his emotions. You could almost say he threw major tantrums and Momma took the brunt of them. The first time I can recall one of his tantrums and then hearing "*it*" happen, I was probably 5 or 6 years old. The "it" was indicative of the horrific behavior Dada displayed towards Momma. I remember being in bed this particular, but I wasn't asleep. I remember there was a night light across the room that gave off a soft, dim glow strangely making me feel safe. The *safe* feeling faded quickly. That night I heard noises; strange, muffled noises coming from outside my bedroom. Suddenly I felt anything but safe. In fact, I was terrified. I remember thinking, *"What is happening?" "Are Momma and Dada ok?"* I wanted Momma to come into my room and hug me tightly. I needed her to protect me but, she couldn't even protect herself. Suddenly, I could hear Dada trying loudly to convince Momma (once again) to forgive yet another “*hiccup*.” He’d cheated. He screamed and begged and pleaded. His tone was surprisingly different and made me very frightened. I didn’t understand most of what he said during their exchange but then it all stopped. Now, I didn’t hear anything. I wanted to go to the door and open it to see what was happening, but I was frozen in place. I was terrified. I could hear loud thumping, bumping, and faint whimpering outside my bedroom door, and I didn’t know what that meant. I could also hear Dada’s voice but it was muffled. I remember crying softly, tears streaming down my cheeks and saturating my pillow. I wanted to yell out “STOP!” “Please Dada make it STOP! STOP it now!” But I was afraid. I didn’t like hearing Dada this way. My innocent little 5- or 6-year-old mind couldn’t comprehend then what I would come to fully understand in the years that followed. All I knew in that moment was something being said between the two of them was intense and I couldn’t hear it. What came next would stay with me, forever. “*It*” happened. “SMACK. SMACK. SMACK. SMACK.

SMACK." Silence. I was frozen and I wanted so badly for Momma to come to me, to protect me, to tell me everything was ok. It may have only been a few seconds before my bedroom door finally opened, but it felt like hours. The creaking sound the door always made became magnified with nervous anticipation. I pulled the cover over my head because I was completely panicked. Who was it? What was that smacking sound? Was I having a nightmare? It was Momma. She came in and slowly sat down on my bed. I couldn't see her because I still had the covers over my head, but I could hear her breathing. I could feel her labored, withered breathing. She was quietly sobbing. Through the sobs, she slowly pulled the covers back to reveal my terrified little face, wet from my tears. She leaned into me, slowly but surely, and pulled me close to her. Her face was hot. Her cheeks were wet with tears. She sobbed harder and rocked me in her arms. I was no longer crying for me, now I was crying for Momma. She seemed different at that moment but

I couldn't know in what way. Not until many years later would I understand how she was different.

It would be several years later before "*It*" would happen again. Momma and Dada would go on and live and love each other in their fractured way. Thinking back on it, for a 5- or 6-year-old it's hard to process why something like this would happen between two people that you love. The two people that introduce you to and are the role models for all of your "firsts." First time crawling, first time sitting up, first step, first word, first food, first day of school, first embrace, first kiss, first love. All the *firsts* are shared with these two people if you're lucky. And I was. But there were so many things that were not quite right. And some "firsts" I didn't need or deserve to know. So how lucky was I, really?

Soon it was no longer just me, there was another person added to the lucky/unlucky equation. Lenox Josiah Timmons was born on a blazing hot summer day in June of 1981. My baby brother. He was so cute and fat. Hell, he was a big ass baby. I mean big. Momma said he was as heavy as a bag of white russet potatoes, to put it into context for me. Lenny, as I called him, was a happy boy, with curly black hair, full chubby cheeks, and very fair skin. I was thrilled to have someone with me even though he was several years younger than I was. I doted over him like he was my baby. I'd sit with Momma and beg to feed him or change his diaper. She would always humor me, letting me do little things here and there but soon those became things I could actually help her with. And I loved every minute of it. I would hear him crying from my room and run down the hallway to the nursery to scoop him up. Momma had to be there to help because, for a long time, I couldn't reach into the crib. But then she'd hand him to me and let me be. I would sing to Lenny and he would always smile. He always had the biggest smile for me. I'm sure he did the same for Momma and Dada but I pretended he only smiled for me. Our bond was unmistakable. I needed him and he needed me. As the years forged on, Lenny and I would do everything together. Despite our differences in age, Momma and Dada made sure to keep us connected in every way.

Lenox Josiah Timmons is a gentlemen's gentleman. He is kind, considerate, handsome, ambitious, and intelligent. I worry about him sometimes because his kindness is often mistaken for weakness. It's been that way since he was a little boy. I'd have to come to his rescue with the bullies at school but not in the way that you think. He suppresses his emotions but actually has a quiet storm raging inside and when pushed hard enough, he explodes like an atomic bomb. So, when he was younger, the boys initially thought he was an easy mark and tried to intimidate him. That's when I'd typically step in to warn them that they'd better be cautious about how hard they pushed. This one little jackass kid, named Benjamin Jeffries, kept antagonizing Lenny. He'd knock Lenny's books out of his hands, trip him in the hallway, throw spitballs at him, etc. and Lenny would just brush it off, barely reacting to it most of the time. But Benji was relentless; you know, he was the type that had to get a crowd to gather around. Well, this particular day while they were walking home from school he kept coming for Lenny, taunting him and becoming increasingly physical. My friend Karla found me back on school grounds and told me what was happening so I rushed to the scene as quickly as I could. But by the time I'd reached the growing crowd, Lenny was whaling on Benji with everyone screaming and egging it on. Lenny was beating the shit out of Benji. All of Benji's friends stood back, and not one person jumped in. I pushed through and grabbed Lenny from behind dragging him away with all my might. His face was red as a beet, and he looked as if he was in a trance. He was still punching, kicking, and swinging his arms with tears streaming from his eyes. I was trying to calm him down but all he kept saying is "Now what, Now what??!!" That's that "*quiet storm*". He completely blacks out and it's hard to reach him when he gets that way. It took me almost 20 minutes to get him to chill the fuck out. Karla had run to our house to get Dada and of course, he rushed to come to see what was going on. Thankfully, we were only a few blocks away from our house. I remember walking to the car in silence and then sitting in the backseat with Lenny rubbing his legs, because they were trembling. Dada was going off on us and I was baffled. He said, "I cannot believe I had to be told to come gather my children who were behaving like animals." In my mind, I was thinking, *"Dang, what did I do? I was trying to protect and control my brother"*. But in Dada's mind, we were both behaving in a manner that was unlike anything he would ever condone. He expected us to stand up for ourselves for sure, but we should always use logic, never our hands. The irony in that expectation was astounding to me, especially coming from Dada. For the rest of the ride home, no one spoke, and the silence was deafening. As we sat on opposite sides of the backseat, tears streamed down my and Lenny's cheeks, in tandem. My tears fell because I could feel Dada's disappointment in my behavior. I never wanted to let him down. In my eyes, he was the hero. He is infallible; even knowing what I knew. Despite all the things he'd done, he has always been my hero. On the flip side, I'm positive that Lenny's tears were the result of absolute rage. Perhaps partly aimed at Benji and Dada. Likely more towards Dada. Lenny had seen and experienced some of the same episodes that I had. How many times can a boy see his father lay hands on his mother and it does not have an effect on him? Unlike me, however, Lenny would always intervene. He wouldn't, he couldn't just stand there or hide under the covers like I had so many times before. Without question and oftentimes without warning, we would experience a flood of disappointment, tears, and consequently rage as it would be revisited time and time for me, Lenny, Momma, and even Dada. Life has its way of reminding us that there are many things we can control, but equally many more things that we cannot. The reality of this notion strikes you like a thunderbolt when you forget which is which.

Two: **Façade**

~a false appearance that makes someone or something seem more pleasant or better than they really are~

-2-

The adolescent years were a struggle for me, especially that transition from preteen to teen. I was so uncertain about who I was and who I wanted to be. I spent most of my time trying to fit in rather than finding and figuring out the things that made me happy. I remember in high school; I squeezed in rather easily with the "in" crowd and skated along as if I belonged; but deep down, I knew I did not. Most of the time I was uncomfortable in my skin and often mimicked what I saw and heard. No one could see that though, and in actuality, it was so weird and extremely stressful for me. It was all bullshit but I mastered the ability to fake it. I felt like I was always waiting for someone to call me out and say, *"Why is she here?"* I would dress like the other girls, usually in ways that weren't quite my style. I would comb my hair like them and walk and talk like them. I'd get high, I'd get drunk, I'd cut class, I'd do all the things that weren't naturally my things to do. The only time I felt like myself was when I was alone, listening to music and painting. I would literally lose time when I sat in front of a canvas. The way it felt to hold the paintbrush and use the paint to create images came so naturally to me. I would pour out my feelings on the canvas, for hours. The painting was a safe haven for me. It was freeing and innately my thing. But trust me, these girls I hung out with weren't into art or music or really anything of real substance. If so, no one knew it because they didn't talk about it. They spent the majority of their time trying to "one up" the other when it came to fashion, getting high, and doing nasty things with boys. That was the area that really gave me heartburn and anxiety. I wasn't experienced with boys at all. But because of the ways these girls behaved and the ways they spoke about their experiences, I would chime in with these fake detailed ass stories about what I had done, what I would do, or who I would do. Speaking in this way did spark an interest in me that made me really curious. My imagination was vivid but I knew in time, I'd have to present real proof of something and that scared the shit out of me. When the girls got together I'd sit and listen to their stories and work hard to keep my mouth closed from the shock. Most of what they talked about was unbelievable and pretty disgusting. I didn't want to do most of what they were doing; but I admit I was curious. I mean, what does it feel like to have someone lick on your neck or suck your tongue? I imagine it's wet and warm. But then what happens? Do you wipe it away or spit or swallow it? I just had no clue but I'd sit there with my "*oohs*" and "*ahhs*" and "*aw hell yeah girl*" like the other girls, cheering the storyteller on. One girl talked about her guy touching her all over, lifting up her bra and massaging her nipples. She said she felt herself getting wet (*down there*). My eyes were bucked out of their sockets. Then she said he started sucking all over her body and she showed us the results. She was really fair skinned so the marks on her body looked more like bruises than anything that would bring someone pleasure. I was stunned, it looked painful as hell. She swore it felt amazing. I had to fight the urge to say "*girl are you okay*" because she looked like someone had beat her ass! She went on to tell us that they "did it." THEY. DID. IT. I couldn't contain my embarrassingly obvious amazement but this time I wasn't alone. Every one of us sat there with a look of astonishment on our faces as she began to describe in detail what happened between them. She said that once the body sucking was over, he slowly began to put his fingers inside her panties and started touching her "*down there*." She said she moaned in pleasure and felt herself getting wetter and wetter. She described how her eyes were closed for most of it but every now and then she would open an eye slightly. She could see his face; he looked so serious and focused. It made her even more wet. I didn't fully understand the notion of "getting wet". In my mind, I was thinking she might have been peeing on herself. But that didn't make sense. I shook my head as if to shake the stupid thought away. Then I felt myself squirming as she continued to share the details and quickly glanced to see how the other girls were responding. It was clear the reaction I was having was a shared experience. Every one of the girls was shifting slightly in her seat. She then said he put a finger inside her and she winced in pain at first but then felt a rush in her body and then a warm feeling. *It's pee*, I said in my head. Someone bumped against me, which led me to realize I'd actually said it out loud and not in my head. She went on to say he whispered in her ear and asked if she liked it and wanted more. She said yes. At that moment I swear I heard myself say yes too, and then I coughed softly to kind of play it off. *Why am I reacting in this way?,* I thought. So then, she said, he put in another finger, and she yelped out loud. He laughed softly and began kissing her neck, then her breasts. He removed his hand from inside her and began taking off her clothes. At this point our mouths were wide open, we were hanging on to every word. I felt my armpits getting wet from perspiration. *What is happening*?, I thought. She then said she helped him remove her clothes. He then took off his clothes and climbed on top of her. She said it was hot and they were both sweating. When he entered her, she was afraid and in some discomfort, but he kept whispering in her ear to assure her that she was going to be okay. This all sounded like something from a movie that I would've sneaked to see because of the X-rated scenes; but it was real, at least she had us believing it was. Once he was inside her she described them moving back and forth in a fast then slow manner. She said it *felt good as hell.* Those were her words. I hung on to everything she said, and my curiosity was now out of control. There was something about the fact that I knew her that made it real for me too. We were all sitting there, mesmerized by her story. Some of the girls were openly expressing themselves and some of us were simply in some kind of hypnotic trance. When she finished telling her story, I felt mentally overstimulated and felt like I needed to leave. I was hot and strangely bothered by their presence all of a sudden. I had no idea why I became so overstimulated, but I needed to get out of there immediately. We all strangely laughed in unison perhaps from nervousness or not being sure what we should say or do. But then I made up some excuse about needing to get home and I left. As I walked home, my mind was racing with the thoughts of what I'd just heard. The summer breeze wasn't having its usual calming effect on me. I felt agitated and restless. When I got home, I had this weird sensation come over me; it was something I hadn't experienced before. Momma was in the kitchen when I got home, and she was saying something to me, but I don't even recall what. Her mouth was moving but I was completely distracted by what I was experiencing in my body so I didn't hear a thing she said, and then I quickly excused myself. I remember her calling my name but I went into my bedroom, closing the door. I was pacing in circles. I was really warm all over so I took off my pants and got into the bed, covering myself completely. I used to do this when I was little; get into bed and cover myself completely from head to toe. But this time was different. I closed my eyes and I began replaying the things my friend said. I felt myself smile a bit, then I began touching myself down there. I had never done this or felt this way in my life and it kind of scared me, but I didn't stop. Her story came to life in my mind and I touched myself in the ways she described. One finger inside. Slow at first. Then another finger. In and out. In and out. I was so wet and confused by what was happening, but I liked it. A lot. I moved around in my bed under those covers for what felt like hours. Exploring the places on my body I had never explored before. Soft muffled moans, oohs and aahs escaped me as I searched out the places on my body that gave me the most satisfaction. I was pleasuring myself and it felt amazing. I heard a knock on the door and then the knob slowly turned. It was Momma. She poked her head in, "Lena girl, you feeling okay?" she asked. At first, I didn't respond. I was too concerned with the possibility that she may have heard me. Then I peeked my head from under the covers and said, "Yeah Momma, I'm ok. It's just cramps." She told me to take a hot shower and a couple of Tylenol, then reminded me where I could find the heating pad. I thanked her and she closed the door. I was shaking all over, unclear if it was due to the exhilaration I was feeling from my *pleasure* exercise or the nervousness of almost getting caught. Maybe it was both. At any rate, I was feeling good. And I wanted more.

Several weeks had passed and I didn't dare mention my experience to the girls. I mean what do I say? "*Hey y'all, the reason I left that day was because I got turned on by the story and went home to play with myself?*" Mind you, these girls weren't prudes at all and likely would've gotten a kick out of it, but *this* topic hadn't come up in any of the conversations they'd shared before. No one was telling their dirty tales of touching themselves in the privacy of their homes. In my mind, I think I was still in shock, but my curiosity was growing. I wanted something more. I hadn't felt this certain about anything ever, outside of my love for art. Without question, I needed to and desired to explore this feeling, this new sense of pleasure and excitement. These feelings are in stark contrast to what had been hammered into my head as a young girl. Momma had always shared her personal beliefs about virginity and taught me about the importance of saving myself for true love. She'd say, '*Boys will be about nothing more than getting into your panties if you let them.*' She'd bring it home with a statement like, '*The world doesn't need no fatherless, bad ass kids from a broken home, cause these niggas will leave you alone to take care of a baby faster than you can blink an eye, you hear me?*' I believed her and held on to that belief for the better part of my teenage years but after several sessions of the "*pleasure experience,*" something in me shifted. What I wanted had nothing to do with having a baby. I would be careful. But I wanted to be with someone, to connect in that way. To be touched that way. I had to. I didn't have a boyfriend or anything but I knew several guys at school were kind of into me. I found myself kinda digging on them as well, but I never allowed anything to come of it. Gentle flirting here and there, a handhold or a playful hug in the hallway between classes, but nothing more. I had been afraid of it and I also didn't want the label that came with it. I heard the things being said about the other girls. I didn't want to be spoken of in that way. I cared about my reputation. But after what I'd done. I was curious. I was anxious. I was ready.

One evening after one of our home football games, the crew and I went to a party. Everyone was there, the jocks, cheerleaders, stoners, house heads, thugs.... any and every one you can think of. The girls and I were sitting together with a few guys we knew, laughing and talking shit. This was our Senior year and we were the "*shit*." Everyone wanted to either *be* us or *be with* us. Suddenly one of the guys said something like, "*Damn Lena, what's up wit' you, you out here looking all fly and shit*?" I was flattered by the compliment but played it off. "*Boy, shut up*!" I said, laughing under my breath. "*Nah for real, what's up*?" he said, "*My guy been checking you out, he over there*." I looked over to where he was pointing to see this tall, handsome dude smiling at me. I smiled in return. He started walking over and I instantly felt warm and fidgety, which must have been obvious to my girls cause they all started laughing. I shot a look at them that clearly indicated

"*PLEASE STOP IMMEDIATELY*," but they kept laughing. "*Bitches*!" I thought in my head. Next thing I knew he was standing in front of me. Someone pushed me from behind and I stood up to avoid falling off the sofa's edge. He grabbed my arm, and I got warm again. "Hey," I said. He smiled harder. *Damn, this dude is foine as hell* I thought, praying I hadn't just said it out loud. "Hey back at you," he responded. I smiled. We stood there like some goofballs smiling for at least a minute. Then he leaned down to my ear and whispered, "Lena, right?" So, at this point, the warmth in my body felt like literal steam coming from my nostrils and ears. I felt like people could see it. "Lord help me," I was saying in my head (at least I hope it was in my head). "Yes, it's Lena," I replied coyly. Now please understand, I'd seen him many times before at basketball games, he was on the team, but I only knew his player number. It was 6, which just so happens to be my favorite number. He leaned in again and said, "I'm Ty, Ty Walters." I looked up into his eyes, which were a deep warm brown and he had a dimple in his right cheek.... “Lord have mercy,” I said. This time out loud.

Ty and I had a whirlwind romance from the moment we connected. That first night we spoke ignited a flame in us that burned like molten lava. We were inseparable and my family loved him. He grew up in a two-family home, like me, and his parents were educators. His father, Theo, was a professor at one of the top universities in downtown Chicago and his mother, Tiffany, was a principal at an elementary school in Hyde Park. He had 4 siblings, three older brothers and one brother younger than him. The boys all had names that began with the letter T; they are Tristan, Timothy, Tobias, Ty, and Tucker. Them damn Walters’ boys are all smart and fine as hell. But if you asked me, Ty is THEE finest one of the bunch!

I fell hard for Ty and everything about his family structure was attractive to me. They seemingly had a picture-perfect family dynamic. Hard working, educated parents, smart, athletic and handsome children. And they were very down to earth. His entire family opened up to me in a way that immediately made me feel like I was a part of their clan. I had keys to the house, drove their cars, went to all the reunions. Everything was just amazing. Almost too amazing at times. But I took it all in and above all else I was head over heels in love with Ty. I would do anything for him and he knew it. I felt the same way about him. For a very long time there was no reason for me not to believe that he was the one. No reason at all. We connected in every way. He could make me laugh, we could talk about anything, our families loved us both. The first time we kissed I swear I felt as though I would literally melt. There was a passion between us that was unreal. When we made love for the first time I cried. The way he touched me and took his time with me was so erotic. It wasn't long after we'd first met when it happened. In fact, it was about 3 weeks later. It was after one of his games and the whole crew was out together celebrating the big win. Ty was on cloud nine after the game, this had been a long hard fight. This team had kicked our team's ass consistently in the last several years and it was anticipated that this game wouldn't be any different. It was a nail biting, buzzer beatng win, but it was a win, nonetheless. Ty had shot the ball for the winning point and the gym erupted. I was so proud of my man. I screamed so long and hard that I'd almost completely lost my voice. We all met up at our friends' house later to celebrate and I'd never seen Ty so amped up. I remember dancing with my girls and then someone grabbed me from behind. I turned around and it was Ty. He said, "let's go." I motioned to my girls and we were out the door heading to Ty's car. Once inside the car, he pulled me to him and began kissing me hard on my mouth. We loved to kiss and we kissed all the time. But this time he was so aggressive. Not in a way that felt forceful but it felt intense. He pulled away from me and said, "I want you." I felt my whole-body shudder and my panties were getting wet. I said, "I want you too baby." He started the car and we were off. I wasn't sure where to but it didn't matter. I was trembling inside partly from the anticipation of what I felt was about to happen and partly from fear of the same thing. In either case, I wanted it to be with Ty. Period. No questions asked. He pulled into the driveway of his house and we sat there for a few minutes. Neither of us said a word at first. Then he grabbed me and pulled me close kissing my neck and whispered, "let's go inside." The lights were off and I knew no one was home. That night after the game his family went straight to their summer house in Indiana for the weekend. Ty and I were going as well, but not until the next day. It was almost as if they knew what was going to happen that night. It couldn't have been more perfect.

Ty and I walked inside and he said, "I'm gonna go take a shower…you coming?" I froze. Did I hear him right? He walked into the kitchen, grabbed a soda from the fridge and then asked me again, "Babe, you coming?" This time I said "Yes" but it was soft I wasn't sure he'd heard me. I guess he had heard me because as he walked past me he grabbed my hand and we went upstairs. I was freaking out.

We walked into his bedroom and I sat on the edge. Ty calmly went into the bathroom, started the shower, and then came back into the bedroom. He took a sip of his soda and placed it on the dresser. Then he walked over to me, stooping down in front of me. He slowly began taking my sneakers off, one by one. Then he slid my socks off. He stood up and pulled me up off the bed. He leaned in and kissed me softly on my neck, then my ear then my cheek and finally landed on my mouth. He stuck his tongue in my mouth and we kissed for what seemed to be forever. It was so good and long and passionate that I didn't even realize he was pulling my shorts off. Next, he was caressing me all over my back and then my butt with slow, soft, intentional strokes. I was so wet. He unfastened my bra and pulled my tee shirt over my head. Kissing me gently with every move he made. Damn, I loved him. He made me feel so good, safe, and sexy. Ty took off his shorts and tee shirt and we were both standing there. Naked. I had never done this before but with Ty it felt natural. It felt right and I wanted more. He grabbed my hand and we walked into the bathroom which was steamed up from the shower. Ty scooped me up and placed me on the bathroom sink. We stared into each other's eyes as I straddled his body and he said again, "I want you". He leaned into me, licking my neck and stopping at my ear, then whispered, "You ready?" I nodded yes, and we got in the shower. The water was running over us but I couldn't tell you if it was burning hot or freezing cold. All I knew was my body was hot and wet and ready for whatever came next. Ty kissed me all over my body. ALL OVER MY BODY. He got down on his knees and his tongue went to work on my *cookie*. It was throbbing. It was ready for him. I grabbed his head to brace myself. I had never been able to make myself feel the pleasure he made me feel. He worked me out until I let out a yelp and then he stood up to kiss me on the mouth. I could see my wetness all over his face. I knew it was from me because it looked different from the water droplets. Initially, I was kind of grossed out but I didn't stop him. It all had felt so damn good that nothing mattered to me at that moment. He was so intentional that I quickly let go of the reservations I'd had a few minutes earlier. I loved him. He loved me. That's all I cared about. We kissed and groped and poked and prodded for several minutes. He then grabbed the soap and lathered my body all over, in tandem with his own. We rinsed and quickly got out of the shower. I felt like I was in some strange state of euphoria, my body was tingling. I was beyond content with what had just happened because I had never felt that way and couldn't imagine what could feel better. Well, Ty knew. I was too inexperienced to understand that there was more to come. We dried off and walked back into the bedroom. I was still wrapped in the towel and was just about to reach for my underwear when Ty grabbed me and said, "What you doing babe, we just getting started." Before I could even respond, he had laid me on the bed and started kissing me hard, tongue deep in my mouth. I felt his hands moving all over me and then he put a finger inside me. My body shuddered and the moisture was back.

Then another finger went inside me. Ty was like a ravenous, wild animal. He was breathing hard, heavily, and moaning low; hell, so was I at this point. He started sucking my breasts and I thought I was about to lose it. I had never been able to make myself feel this way. I felt as though I was going to explode. Then I felt Ty adjust himself to where he was now eye to eye with me and felt something hard, hot, and large between my legs. He was slowly entering me. I cried out a little because it hurt but strangely it also felt good. I kept my gaze on Ty the entire time. Then I heard him say, "Aw shit." Followed by, "You ok baby?." Then, "Shhhhhhhhit you feel so damn good." It felt like I was in a dream, and we were moving in slow motion. Then fast motion. Then slow motion again. No further words were spoken but it was definitely noisy in the room from all the moans and cries and slapping sounds coming from our bodies. Ty never took his eyes off me and I was mesmerized. I felt excited and at ease and tense and nervous and scared all at the same time. "This is crazy," I said to myself. But I didn't want it to end. Ty was my first. It was nothing like I could have imagined but everything I could have ever wanted. We went at it for two hours straight. My body had strange reactions, my *cookie* was sore as hell and I was sweating everywhere. I learned so many things about myself and him for that matter. We explored each other's bodies and pleasured each other in ways that would shame the devil. It was almost unnatural for two teenagers to have this much passion for one another. For me, it was a combination of curiosity and intense lust. We took time to nurture our desires and subsequently nurtured one another.

Time and life marched on and we learned that love wasn't always enough. In college, Ty became this mega basketball star and the impact of all the attention began to weigh heavily on our ability to sort out the issues that we faced. Most of the issues centered around the attention he'd receive from the groupies. To be clear, I wasn't naïve to think that he wouldn't be sought out, or even sought after. But for Ty and me, this attention spiral became littered with episodes of deceit and broken promises. And it was just the beginning of a long winding road of heartbreak, lies, and the deepest betrayal imagined.

Three: **Freak**

~behave or cause to behave in a wild and irrational way~

-3-

"Ty Walters!." "Aye, yo! What up Ty?" "Can I get a picture?" I would hear these requests every time we went anywhere. It didn't matter whether we were on campus or in the mall. Everywhere we went Ty was pulled away to appease some fan's request. In the beginning, I kind of enjoyed the attention he'd get; almost envied it on some small level. But mostly it felt good to be on the arm of "THEE" Ty Walters, star basketball player at Morgan State University. Ty had received a full-ride athletic scholarship and I was enrolled in their College of Sciences with a dual focus in Biology and Clinical Psychology. Morgan State was on the list of potential schools I considered attending but it wasn't my first choice. I had always talked about going to an HBCU and Spelman was my top choice. I'd had several friends, and relatives who attended before me and when I visited the campus I was so amazed by the beautiful black women and girls on campus. There was a distinct and undeniable energy that you felt the moment you walked onto the campus. I wanted to be a part of that. I wanted to be able to say I was part of a rich history and legacy. I'd actually been accepted to several of the top HBCU's. Howard, Hampton, and FAMU. I was also accepted to several state schools, which my parents preferred I choose. Loyola, Roosevelt University, and University of Chicago all accepted me and I'll admit I was on the fence about U of C, but a huge factor in my decision was Ty. Momma and Dada were not happy about that at all. There were many arguments, slammed doors, and crying leading up to the moment I *had* to make the final decision. And somehow, I won the fight. I guess they figured they'd rather concede to let me follow my heart and not force me to do what they wanted. Having a broken and lonely heart would certainly impact me and cause my head to not be in the game at all. That's what I thought not being with Ty meant. That I wouldn't be able to focus. That I wouldn't be able to do the things I'd planned to do, because he wasn't there. This man had me wrapped around his finger and he knew it. And I was good for him. I held him together on many levels. No one, and I mean no one, could have ever told me that at the end of it all he would manipulate me with sex and lies. But he did. I fell for it. I followed him. I believed in the fantasy of it. And I paid a lofty price.

The first semester at Morgan State was really, really tough for me. I was completely distracted, almost felt like I was outside my body. I had a hard time being away from home. I missed my family desperately. Despite my parents' strong feelings and repeated warnings about going to Morgan State, I had convinced myself that going to the same school with my "man" would lessen the notion of being homesick and that I would be able to keep it together. Wrong. The first week or so I was taking things in stride, as it pertained to my classes. I spent an inordinate amount of time trying to plan out my courses and general schedule. I wanted to be sure I'd gotten the names of my professors written down and aligned the syllabus to each of them. That was my way, always over-prepared, and overthinking. I was really trying to dig deep into my studies but instead found myself knee-deep in all things concerning Ty. Running errands for him, making sure he got to where he needed to be, and at times, even doing "his" work. Girl, like what the hell? I mean, don't misunderstand, he was super busy. The school constantly had him in motion. Most of his time was spent hanging with the team, running workouts, watching film, or going out on campus partying with his teammates. Meanwhile, despite all the planning and prepping I'd done, I was out of sorts and my first semester grades reflected it. I don't even know or remember when things with school went completely off the rails, although there were several times when I'd wake up and Ty would be gone... off to the places he needed to be or to meet the person he needed to meet. There was little to no consideration given to what I needed or where I needed to go. The balance of effort and attention didn't level out, I didn't take heed to that. I let it go and didn't say things that might incite an argument. I never said things. Ever. I just went along with it. Pleasing him. Always.

By the second semester, my parents were threatening bodily harm to me if I didn't get my shit together so I tried to focus my efforts on my needs as best I could. I met with my academic advisor, and we came up with a very detailed plan to get me back on track. I ended the first semester so poorly that talks about yanking my scholarship were in motion and that would have sealed my fate and concluded my time at Morgan State. Momma and Dada thankfully had some friends in high places and were able to get them to agree to allow one last semester to get it right. So, there was very little room for bullshit. But sooner than not I came to understand that bullshit was getting ready to take up full residency in my life.

Ty and I were seemingly in an *okay* place. Seemingly. Nothing was wrong, but nothing was really right either. We just "were". He was busy all the time and trying hard to live up to the superstar status he'd been recruited to Morgan State for. He was always in practice. Then off to watch film. Then off to go watch another school's team play. Then off to meet with Coach and so on and on-and blah, blah, blah. I knew his schedule inside and out, though I was not certain if he ever knew or cared fully about mine. But we would carve out time to hang out to catch up, do a little snuggling here and there, and whatever else, as time and effort would permit. It became very robotic. Ty was living his best life, and it was truly his cause it sure as hell wasn't mine. I would sit, and watch, and wait, for him. Constantly. I was losing myself in him. In whom he was becoming. In whom he was shining his light for. I knew it, my friends knew it, my parents knew it. But unlike them, I didn't care. The way I felt about Ty, I would go to the ends of the earth for him, at any cost. He had *that* kind of hold on me. And while I didn't always feel the same effort from him, he never let me down physically. Our connection and our chemistry were unmatched.

After one of the away games, we'd gotten back to campus and he was immersed in the afterglow of a big win. I would usually stand in the parking lot, fall back, and watch the groupies, the teammates, the coaches vie for his attention. People knew that I was his girl but I never boasted or showboated for that attention, even though I could have done a much better job of commanding or demanding respect from them all. In my mind, though, none of that mattered. I wasn't intimidated by the chicks that stood outside the locker room or waited in the parking lot when the team bus would pull up waiting for the players to deboard. When Ty walked off the bus these broads would lose themselves, screaming, reaching, groping, grasping for any little bit of him. His buddies would sometimes see me and throw a smile or smirk my way. They knew I didn't give a shit about any of that. They knew I knew what I had in Ty, so I would fall into the background. He was leaving with me. So, after this one particular game, once the coach let them go, he finally made it to me in the parking lot and we got into his car. Usually, I would drive but this day he insisted. We pulled off and I was about to ask how he was feeling, if he was sore, and if he wanted a good massage. We approached the traffic light just as it turned red. He said, “Take off your panties.” Perhaps someone else’s response would have been “Huh?” or “Why?” but I didn’t say anything. I knew that tone he’d used so I simply did as I was told. We drove for another 15 minutes or so and he reached over to stick his fingers inside me. I opened my mouth and let out a gasp and Ty said “Sssshhhhhhhhhhhhh.” Then he said, “The more you moan, the deeper I go.” Maybe he thought that was a threat to me because I moaned, with intention. And like he said, he went deeper. And with every moan, he went deeper and deeper. I was so lost in the pleasure that I hadn’t realized that we had pulled into the parking lot of a golf course. It was a warm summer night and the sun was close to setting. There was a glazed color in the sky like orange and red with hints of grey. We parked and he lingered inside me for a while longer. Then he put his fingers in his mouth, licking me off of every finger and said, “Get out.” We were near the driving range and I asked, “Why are we here babe?” I looked around to see if there were any people nearby because I knew Ty was up to something. He said, “Go to the bench and wait there.” Again, I looked around because now I wanted to be certain there was no one around. “What is he up to?” I thought but I was so wet, throbbing and ready it didn’t matter. I was sitting for a few minutes when I felt Ty suddenly standing behind me. He ran his hands down my shirt and lightly touched my breasts. Then he bent over me pulled up my skirt and spread my legs apart, gently running his fingers inside me again and putting them in his mouth. This went on for several minutes and then walked around to the front of the bench and sat next to me. He told me to stand up. I did. Then he told me to stand on the bench with one foot on either side of him making me stand over him, almost hovering. He raised my skirt up over his head and gripped my bare butt cheeks. He buried his face in my *cookie* and all I felt was the intense suction of his lips taking me in. He parted my lips with his tongue and explored me right there on the driving range of the local golf course. My head fell backward from the pleasure-zoned place I was in and if Ty did not have a tight grip on me like he did, I would have fallen backwards. His mouth was so warm and wet and so was I. We stayed in this stance for what felt like forever and then all of a sudden a bright flood of lights beamed over us. The sun had set and it got dark enough for the course lights to come on. If anyone had been on the greens they would have definitely seen and heard some things. I think we both noticed the lights, but Ty didn't stop. Ty and I always seemed to have to vocal plaything between us when we fucked. We got loud. He sucked and licked me until my legs went limp. He flung me over his shoulder and took me to the middle of one of the fairways where he laid me down and entered me. Slowly, gently, and repeatedly. On the 4th hole of the golf course on the fairway greens under the glaring lights, Ty and I made love.

Time after time, that would become our pattern. I would spend the predominance of my week in classes, Ty would spend his time in classes and then in practice. The in-between would be spent entwined in some freaky escapade. We would always go someplace new, always after the games. He would take me away and it would be our special time. I was so used to the pattern that I didn't notice much else. Ty had a way of hypnotizing me through sex that the other issues brewing below the surface of our relationship were slowly beginning to bubble up and I didn't even notice. Time went by and Ty and I had so many off-campus sexcapades that I'd lost count. Our sex life was intense and had always left me completely mesmerized and fixated on him. Anything he wanted from me; he could get, always. It was always us, always. He loved on me and treated me like I was the only thing that mattered to him, always. He made me feel safe when I was with him, always. That is until I was hit by what would become the biggest shock to my system, always.

Homecoming games at Morgan State were a huge deal for the students, alumni, staff and most especially for the players. The hype was unlike anything you could imagine. The parties, the pep rallies, the cheerleaders, the band, the connections were unmatched. It was all part of the experience and everyone at Morgan State was on "10" this particular year. I began to notice that Ty was distracted when he was with me for some reason. I assumed it was just the build-up to and anticipation of the big game. He would usually become a bit preoccupied but something was noticeably off and it was worrying me. The night of the game, my girls and I were getting ready and pregaming. We'd been listening to music and sipping vodka cocktails when I heard my girl Kyla on the phone talking to her boyfriend Josh. He played Trombone in the band and was typically practicing so they didn't get to spend a lot of time together these days, especially before the big game. I could tell their conversation was intense, so I mentioned it to our other girl, Ava. Ava was tipsy by this point and dancing in the mirror when she said, “Girl, I heard her cussing his ass out this morning, so this is probably part two.” She laughed a bit and said, “He fucked up big time, I’ll tell you about it later.” Ava loved to be up in everybody’s business and could be “messy” sometimes. She was always telling us the latest and greatest happenings on campus. But I wasn’t really interested in any of that stuff or in what Kyla and Josh had going on. My own shit was shaky as hell and that’s all I cared about. I tried to call Ty four times that morning and he didn’t answer or call me back. “That’s not like him”, I thought to myself. But gameday is stressful and I tried to redirect my thoughts. I also knew that win or lose, we’d go somewhere and *do our thing*. That was our usual pattern. No matter what. I took another gulp of my vodka cocktail when I heard Kyla yell, “Aw hell naw, I’m telling her!! I’m showing this to her right now! What the fuck? Yall ain’t shit!!! He ain’t shit, and don’t call my goddamn number again sick ass nigga!!” Clearly all that got my and Ava’s attention. I put my drink down and Ava turned off the music.

Kyla hung up the phone and walked into the bathroom where we were getting ready and she grabbed some tissue. I assumed it was because she was crying or about to cry. But instead she turned around and handed it to me. I looked at it and then up at her and said, "I don't need this." She said, "Yes, you do. Yes, you will."

I felt like I was dreaming and for some reason my vision was super blurry. I could see, but not clearly. I also couldn't hear anything, it was like there was water in my ears, but I could make out Kyla's mouth was moving. I could also see Ava banging her fist on the bathroom counter as tears streamed down her cheeks. Kyla grabbed my face and pulled me close to hers so I could read her lips. She said, "Lena whatchoo wanna do, whatchoo wanna do???!!!" Ava was still banging her fists on the bathroom counter and saying something to Kyla but I couldn't hear her over the screaming. I stepped away from Kyla and walked out of the bathroom eventually sitting on the edge of the bed. I looked down to see the phone in my right hand. Damn, my vision was so blurred. I looked at it again and I stared for a long time and then my vision miraculously cleared. But I still heard the screaming. There were pictures on the phone. Lots and lots of pictures. I looked closer and could see these were pictures of me. Pictures of me in the various places Ty and I would go after the football games. Pictures of me touching myself, pictures of me giving him head, pictures of me having sex. Ty's face was never shown in the pictures. Only my face was visible. *Who would do this? Oh my God, what would Ty think? Wait, did he do this? No, he wouldn't. He would never. He is gonna fuck up the person that did this shit. How could someone have taken these pictures? Who has seen these?* All these questions were racing through my mind. Then Ava came running up to me and grabbed the phone. She said, "These assholes have been watching you, following you. And he knew Lena. He knew. Ty knew. He did this." She was sobbing. I remember looking at the phone again and then I looked down at my left hand and saw the tissue Kyla had given me earlier. She was standing in front of me again saying something, but I couldn't hear her over the screaming. Who the fuck was screaming??????? It was me. I was screaming.

Four: **Fuck**

~a rude word used when expressing extreme anger~

- 4-

"What the fuck?!!!!!!!!!" That's all I could muster out of my mouth four weeks later. Four long ass weeks later. I'd had a complete mental meltdown in the wake of this bullshit. But with the support of my advisor, school administration, and my select tribe of friends, I was able to make it through these last several weeks to get closer to the end of this horrible semester and horrible nightmare. I called my parents and told them I was going to be coming home for good at the end of the semester. I called my brother and told him I needed him to call *Joe Joe and 'nem* to come up to the campus and break Ty's legs. I wanted to cause serious and permanent physical harm to this motherfucker! I could not believe I was in this place. I could not believe this happened to me. I could not believe I had allowed myself to lose myself in this way. Learning that Ty was capable of and responsible for playing out this sick-ass demented fantasy was more than I would ever be able to understand. I'd found out that he took pleasure in having pictures of us taken while we had sex and paid his friend from the basketball team to follow us. Every fucking time we went to fuck, his sick fucking friend would be waiting somewhere nearby and take fucking pictures of us. Ty would then show the pictures to his teammates, his friends and anyone else who wanted to see them. He would invite them over to see and then he got bold enough to send them out to people in text messages. So, the night of the homecoming game Kyla was in an argument with her guy Josh because earlier that day she walked up behind him and saw a glimpse of a naked girl in his phone. They argued and he made up some bullshit story. Of course, she had no idea, at the time, it was me in the pictures. She was having the normal reaction that any girlfriend would towards her man if something like this presented itself. The more she probed, he quickly removed the doubts she had because she'd never been concerned about anything like this before. But there was something about the way he quickly responded that bothered her. When their conversation continued that evening, she became more and more bothered by his responses and threatened to break up with him. He wasn't going to risk losing her so despite his allegiance to Ty, he told her about the photos and eventually sent them to her. What the fuck????

An investigation ensued and Ty spent more time with school administrators over the last few weeks than he had in his time at Morgan State altogether. Usually, when he was in the Administration building it had something to do with press footage or speaking with the Dean or the Marketing Director about some sports campaign since he was the star player who'd brought on more buzz at Morgan State than anyone had in the last ten years. But these meetings were different and dimmed every bit of his *shine.* The news of what he'd done made it across the campus quickly and I was viewed as the victim in his sick, demented game. It was not a moniker I wore with any sense of pride nor was I interested in the attention it brought on. I was used to just doing my own thing and standing in the background. Before all this chaos, I didn't mind letting him shine. I didn't want or need attention, at least not from anyone but him. That was enough for me. It had always been enough for me. Now I found myself feeling like a scorned wife of some celebrity who got caught up in a salacious incident warranting an interview by Diane Sawyer or Oprah. I could see it now, *"Lena, how did you react when you learned that Ty had done this to you"*, *"What was your initial reaction when you saw the photos"*, *"If you could say anything to Ty what would it be?"* My responses would be the same, *"Fuck, what the fuck and fuck you."* I mean what the fuck else would I say? In reality, he used me, he used his friends and he ultimately fucked himself. Now he and several of his teammates, a handful of members of the band (including Josh), and at least four cheerleaders were being questioned about this. This was a serious offense and he would likely never recover from this. Not fully and certainly not here.

I didn't give a damn about any of it. I just wanted to go home and move on with my life. I felt a heartbreak from this that I would never be able to explain. I loved this man. I trusted this man. We had mapped out our future together. I had finally found a rhythm this semester with my coursework, I'd found a nice job and had some amazing friends. I was proud to be Ty Walters' girl and even though I was never the typical "*over the top, obnoxious*" ball player's girlfriend, people knew who I was. They would always acknowledge me when I'd come to the events, to the games, to the parties. I never sensed anything weird from anyone. We even had friends who were in relationships that we would hang out with. We took trips together during Spring Break and it all seemed normal. Laughing together, cooking, drinking, having fun. But I was clearly the butt of the joke (no pun intended). They knew. The whole time. Every single one of them knew this horrible, horrible thing was happening and said nothing. Fuck 'em! Fuck 'em all!

I was so angry and a scathing bitterness was growing deep inside me as I tried to make it to the end of the semester. Ty had been expelled as were several of the other people involved in this. My friends Ava and Kyla found it hard to be fully present and rarely checked in with me anymore. Kyla's guy Josh was suspended and somehow, he convinced her that staying away from me would be better for them as they worked on repairing what was now a fractured relationship between them. How in the fuck is this my fault???!! What's interesting is, this was becoming a theme on campus. People steered clear of me, you know, the victim. It seemingly became easier to identify me as the problem rather than to support me as I navigated through the problem that presented itself *to me*. I am nothing if not determined so I pushed through my classes, oftentimes sitting alone, and retreating back to my dorm. My professors handled me from afar, I couldn't get office hours with most of them except one. I stopped going anywhere other than to class or to get something to eat. It was a sad and pitiful state of affairs. But the most disgusting thing about all of this is by the end of the semester I had somehow become the problem. One day during the final week of classes, I'd gone to the Administration building to track down the only professor who had shown any sense of care or concern towards me. Her name was Dr. Hilton. I had confided in her one day when she noticed how defeated I looked in class. She tapped me on the shoulder as I was leaving and asked if I was ok. We talked and I confided in her about what had happened and how I'd been made to feel. She offered kindness and compassion and encouraged me to push through. She was a tremendous support to me and I know I wouldn't have made it to the end had she not been there. She knew about my plans to leave at the end of the semester and thought it was best for me to move on with my life. I felt so fortunate to have found her and felt this was the beginning of a new chapter for me. I was feeling a small sense of encouragement and empowerment. It was almost too good to be true. So that day, when I stepped off the elevator and walked towards her office, I could hear her on the phone. Being respectful, I stopped just shy of the door and sat down on the bench in the hallways; but I could still hear her conversation. She said, "Yes, yes, I know. Well, how is he doing? I know this is hard but ya'll just need to hang on for another month or so. This will blow over. I told you she's leaving; this is her last semester. No seriously, she is done at the end of this week to be exact. Poor child, ain't nobody fooling with her no more so I've been playing the caring Professor role and keeping her close. But it's all good. All I want is for my nephew to be back here where he belongs. This is legacy for us. We got a long line of family members that have graced this campus and it won't end over some dumb shit like this. Yeah, I know but Dr. Jameson assured me that once she's gone, the story will die down. Ty can start the appeal process soon after and be back no later than the fall semester. I'm telling you Tiffany, this too shall pass."

I was frozen, I could not move. I could hear her laughing and mocking, all at my expense. She was spinning this shit and trivializing the situation as if there was some "quick fix" for Ty's depravity. I could hear her saying Ty's mom's name over and over. But I could not move. Then something happened. I walked to the door's entrance and stood there as Dr. Hilton kept talking facing the window. I cleared my throat to get her attention and she turned suddenly with a look of both irritation and surprise. She said, "Oh! I need to call you later," and hung up the phone. "Hi, Dr. Hilton," I said smiling slyly. "Hi Lena," she replied cautiously. "How long have you…?" I held my index finger up as if to signal stop. "Long enough. I've been recording you since I walked up and overheard my name and the other disgusting things you said. You've been playing me this whole time. Conspiring with the Walters this whole goddamn time." She stood up and I continued, "Oh no darling stay right there. But let me be clear, I'll expect an "A" in this course you fake ass, lying bitch. Do you think this is a fucking game? You bougie, insensitive assholes are fucking with *my* life! So yeah, run my "A" and then kiss my ass. How dare you play on my trauma like it's nothing. And all for what, to save his sick ass and your LEGACY???!!! Fuck you!! Fuck this school! Fuck Ty Walters! Fuck it all!"

People came into the hallway to see what all the commotion was about. Someone walked up to me and said something that I couldn't make out. I turned and walked to the elevator, sobbing and pressed the down button. When the doors opened I stepped inside and leaned against the back wall to steady myself. I was trembling. As the doors closed I tried calling Ava but my tears were blinding me. I was in shock. When the elevator doors opened at the bottom floor, I slowly walked out of the building and made it to the middle of the quad. Then I just stood there. Someone I knew saw me and asked if was ok. I looked at him and screamed. I screamed for so long and loud I'd lost my voice. Campus security showed up and so did Ava. I was broken and gradually coming undone.

Five: **Fetter**

~something that confines; restraint~

-5-

Life after Morgan State was a blur. The psychological, emotional, and physical stress of it all took a powerful toll on me. I feel like I lost time. I literally cannot remember how I got through those next few years, even up to my graduation from Loyola University. I had enrolled there after leaving Maryland. I was completely traumatized by everything that transpired with Ty. I could barely sleep through the night, rarely ate anything and found it difficult to hold conversation with anyone. But I found myself spending more time managing everyone else's feelings about what had happened and pushing my own feelings about it down. My Dada wanted to kill him and was more worried about what his friends would think. *Ain't that some shit?* My Momma was concerned about any potential impact it might have on her Real Estate deals. *Can you believe that shit?* Lenny was busy managing his friends; there was a lot of chatter amongst his so-called boys and frat brothers. *Niggas ain't shit.* He'd told me that he walked in on a conversation where his boys said they wished they could have gotten hold of the pictures. One guy said, '*Yeah man, shit, Lena fine as hell, I would love to see that ass tooted up in my face! She could get it.*' Lenny was pissed! And that comment had come from one of his closest fraternity brothers. Lenny ran up on him and a shoving match ensued but they were quickly separated. It hurt Lenny to his core and in his heart, he knew the guy was just talking shit. His buddy apologized but there is still some underlying tension. I've personally known this guy since he was a kid but now there's an uncomfortableness when I'm around him. Lenny doesn't bring any of them around as often anymore. It's all just weird; with everyone. Shit.

I can even recall the last encounter I'd had with Dr. Hilton and how hurt I was when I overheard her conversation with Tiffany Walters. When I told my parents, they immediately reached out to an attorney to see if there was any opportunity to sue the school. They went into total protection mode as was expected but there was a huge part of me that preferred they did nothing. I didn't want to have to relive any of this. I'd made it to the end of my journey there and I just wanted to move on. I didn't want any part of some drawn-out legal situation because I'd end up having to face Ty and I couldn't stomach that. I was so broken by it all that the mere thought or mention of his name would literally make me ill. I told my parents that I didn't want to pursue it and that I would come apart if they took it any further. They didn't understand it fully but could see that I was in pain, so against their better judgment, they let it go.

After graduating from Loyola, Summa cum laude I might add, I immediately landed a job as a Mental Health counselor at a well-known non-profit organization in Chicago. The social services industry is stressful as hell, so I needed relief by the end of the week, every week. Being back in Chicago I found myself instantly immersed in all the people, places, and things I thought I'd wanted to escape after graduating high school. I was back in the clubs each weekend from Happy Hour on Fridays to Sunrise on Mondays. Every damn weekend. This pattern began to worry my parents since I was still living with them. They couldn't help noticing that I was unraveling and behaving in a way that was unlike myself. They would see me drag in early on Monday mornings and then wonder how I could pull myself together and go to work. This was not a sustainable practice, and it soon began to wear me down. I was moody as hell and borderline disrespectful, which was not me at all. My brother had had enough of my antics and we got into a heated exchange one evening. I'd come in on a Saturday night to do a quick change of clothing before heading back to hit the streets. My parents and Lenny were sitting in the den watching a movie. When I walked in Dada said, "Wassup baby girl, you joining us? It's one of your favorites...*Legends of the Fall*." I responded, "Uh no thank, don't nobody wanna watch that dry ass shit." My father sat up stunned and Momma put her arm across as if to restrain him, but before he could respond Lenny jumped up. He marched over to me and said, "Who the fuck are you talking to??? Dada was just asking a simple question!" He went on in a more amplified tone, "I'm sick of your moody, unpredictable ass. Everybody is. No one here has done anything to you Lena. All we've done is support you." Something about that last statement triggered me and I snapped. "Supported me???? Are you fucking kidding me?!! If anyone is supporting anyone, it's me supporting y'all!! Is Dada ok?, will Momma's work be affected by what happened?, will Lenny and his boys get back on track?" That shit sits with ME! Every fucking day. All day. I spend more time worrying about ya'll and the impact this situation has had on you rather than the impact it's had on ME!!!! I am tired of it! I'm tired!!! I'm hurt! I'm scared!" By this point crying and hyperventilating but I kept on talking. "This happened to me. ME!!!! I carry the guilt. Every fucking day. I can't escape it. I see it, I think about it and we tip-toe around this motherfucker trying not to pretend like it isn't the big ass black elephant in the room. I try to do the right things all the time and this is something that went horribly wrong. And I can't change that. I went to school, got good grades, and never took drugs, or got pregnant. Then I met a guy, I fell in love with the guy and he betrayed me. He betrayed my trust, he betrayed my belief in men, he betrayed my trust in myself. He destroyed me!!!!! So yeah, now I'm going to go out and live my life away from him and the situation. I don't care about anything more than living my life and living in the moment. I work every fucking day. I don't ask for anything. I don't complain about anything. So don't tell me shit about support, Lenny!!!!! I am going to be reckless, and dance, and drink, and laugh as much as I can goddamn it! Fuck you and your support!!!! I don't want or need it. I'm straight! I'm good! It's all good! I got this. I got me! Fuck it!!!" I turned to walk away and felt a firm grip on my shoulder. I quickly turned around, thinking it was Lenny, and I swung hard landing my whole hand on the side of Momma's face. Dada jumped up and Lenny lunged at me. Momma fell to the floor. Lenny was on top of me and I was swinging wildly. Momma screamed at Lenny to get off of me. She pulled herself up and grabbed me. I fell hard into her chest, sobbing inconsolably. "Momma, Momma, I am so ….. I'm so…. Momma…oh shit." She pulled me in closer and tighter. Then I heard Lenny. He was crying. Then I heard Dada sniffling. We all sat there in the hallway of our house submerged in the sounds of tears and sniffles. No words were spoken. We were all hurting, deeply. But Momma recognized that I was hurting in a way that no one else in this moment would fully understand. All she knew to do was hold me in her arms and let me feel it. All of it.

Several weeks later, I had cut down significantly on partying and drinking. I redirected my focus, time, and energy to my work spending long days with patients, writing case notes, and doing research. I started coming back to myself and needed to because I was on the fast track to becoming one of the lead clinical therapists at the agency. The Clinical Director had already approached me about taking on more saying that it would be a great boost to my professional resume and career trajectory. I was all for it. I was all for anything that would distract me from the random thoughts that continually crossed my mind about what happened and what Ty might be doing now. "*Why the fuck do I care anyway*?" I asked myself. But I did care. I had loved this man. I cared about his well-being and his future; it all truly mattered to me. That hadn't changed. But I shouldn't care. I should want this asshole to hurt as much or more than he'd hurt me. But something wouldn't fully allow me to get to that point. So, I kept myself busy. Abnormally busy.

For the next many months, I would spend long hours at the mental health agency or the library. That was it. I'd work all day and oftentimes run home to change my clothes and then head straight to the library on the campus of the University of Chicago since it was close to home. I would read research article after research article on anything related to mental health disorders in adolescents. I'd read the DSM-5 like it was a best-selling novel that had made it to the New York Times best sellers list. It was not, and it had not. But for a fledgling Clinical Psychologist, this is *the bible*, and I couldn't tear myself away from it. I guess all the hard work and long hours had paid off because what came next was the news I'd wanted and needed to hear.

Dr. Moore, the Clinical Director at the agency, called me to her office one day and said, "I've got some exciting news for you Lena. You've been selected to receive a full scholarship to cover the costs of obtaining your Clinical Mental Health degree." I had already been looking at various Clinical Master's degree programs at Northwestern University, Loyola, and the University of Chicago so this was beyond exciting for me. I squealed and said "Oh my goodness Dr. Moore yes, yes, yes!! Thank you so much for believing in me. You have given me just what I need. You have saved my life!!" She had no idea how true this statement was. She looked at me strangely for a minute and then chuckled. "Oh Lena, my darling, I couldn't think of anyone more deserving of this than you." I rushed over to her and we embraced. I could sense the awkwardness at the moment that we were sharing and even felt her attempts to pull herself away from the embrace, but I couldn't let go.

When I'd said out loud that she had saved my life, I meant it. Over the last several months, I'd felt myself slipping into a deep, dark place. I couldn't shake the low feelings of embarrassment and shame from the "situation." I had been able to successfully mask externally what I was feeling internally but the layers of pain were slowly unfolding. I busied myself with my research and work. I smiled when I got home, ate quickly, and then told Momma and Dada that I was off to the library. I moved like a creature of habit and established a robotic, rhythmic, and repetitive routine. I would have days where I was on an emotional high. And equally have days where I was in a deep, dark funk. I knew what this was, I assessed and diagnosed this behavior all the time. I was clinically depressed. I needed to talk with someone and release. But I mastered the movements. I mastered the dialogue. I mastered the smile. I mastered it all. I mean come on, was on the fast track. I couldn't slow down. If I slow down, then it shows. And I would have to own it. I would have to acknowledge it. I would have to give it room to exist. The pain, the anger, the sadness, the dark thoughts would emerge, it would become a living breathing thing. It would be real. I had no time for that. But at this moment with Dr. Moore, in what was by far one of the happiest moments I'd had in a long while, it was all of a sudden very, very real and it scared the shit out of me.

Not long after receiving the scholarship, I started the Clinical Master's program at The University of Chicago. I excelled so fast in the program that I began to think about keeping the momentum going to continue on and pursue my doctoral degree. Dr. Moore was a strong supporter and had become a mentor to me as I pathed forward in this rigorous program. Despite all the insanity going on in my head most days, I was so proud of myself for being able to maintain a solid A average; especially being among the only three African Americans in the program. I was also the only female. A double whammy! I oftentimes felt like I had a bit of Imposter syndrome, often doubting my ability and capacity to remain in the program. But Dr. Moore and my department Chair, Dr. Jefferson, were amazing cheerleaders for me. I needed it. I was struggling mentally and the closer I got to the "finish line" the more I felt myself coming undone.

One day in my Capstone class, I was getting ready to present a final clinical case with my project team, and I felt a bit strange before we started. I stepped out of the classroom to get some air and walked into the restroom. I stood there looking at myself in the mirror and said, "*Come on girl, you got this. Pull yourself together*." I splashed water on my face, smiled, and walked back into the classroom. My project team consisted of myself and two others from my cohort. We had worked tirelessly on the final project and rehearsed it so many times I'd lost count but we knew this material back and forwards. We were ready. We walked in front of the others in class and Jennifer, my teammate, began to speak. She was about 10 minutes into her part of the presentation, and I began to feel hot. I started fidgeting and moving from side to side. 'Get it together Lena,' I was saying in my head. I began to sweat a bit and thought, *I'm just anxious*. After all, this was a big moment for us. We would be done with our project and the semester would be done. I took a deep breath and forced a fake smile but my mouth was dry as hell. I heard Jennifer say, "And now Lena will speak to you about some new developments with Co-occurring disorders." Jennifer looked over to me and smiled as did Renee, my other teammate. We knew this material and we were halfway through. I walked to the podium and looked down at the monitor. I was frozen in place but I was also extremely hot. My mouth was dry as the desert; it felt like I had a bag of cotton balls in it. I was sweating profusely under my arms and all of a sudden felt as if I were going to pass out. My professor said, "You can start at any time Lena," slightly smiling. I looked at him and my vision became blurry and suddenly I couldn't breathe. I turned to run out of the classroom and that was the last thing I remember.

I woke up to at least four people standing over me. I felt something really cold; it was ice. Jennifer was holding an ice cube against the inner part of my wrist. She was smiling at me with such a caring gaze that I began to cry. I was so embarrassed. I thought in my head,

"I know damn well I did not fall out in the middle of our freaking presentation!!" Our professor walked in with the Nurse and I attempted to stand. "I'm fine, I'm fine," I said softly. I was mortified. I leaned back against the whiteboard with Jennifer and Renee on either side of me. The Nurse asked me a few questions, did a quick assessment, and said you'll be fine Ms. Timmons. This was likely an anxiety or panic attack but I recommend you reach out to your primary care physician. She gave me water and commended Jennifer for knowing the "ice" trick. It's something used to trigger the parasympathetic system when a person is experiencing an event like the one I had. I looked at Jennifer and she winked at me. "I got you, and we got this" she mouthed to me. I smiled and then started to cry again. "How embarrassing! Oh shit, I'm sorry Dr. Witherspoon. I am so sorry about all this." He laughed. "Lena, it's ok." You're not the first person to have this happen. You are all in a very rigorous Clinical program and there is a ton of pressure that comes with that. Don't worry about it. I just want to be sure you're okay and taking care of yourself. Give yourself some grace." He asked if I felt ok to proceed with the rest of the presentation or if we needed an extension. I said, "No, we got this." We completed the presentation, and the semester successfully ended. Unfortunately for me, the panic attacks did not. They were slowly taking hold of me. This was only the beginning.

Six: **Fervor**

~feelings of great warmth and intensity~

-6-

My graduation from the Master's program was a total blur as was most of the next year and a half. I spent a lot of my time travelling. I took off for three months and did a whirlwind tour of Europe and South America. I hopped on every freaking airline that I could as often as I could. A week here, two weeks there. It was all a blur. I met some amazing people, ate amazing things, and danced, danced, danced into the wee hours of the mornings. But when I'd crawl into the bed of these luxurious hotels, a deep heavy sadness came over me and I usually cried myself to sleep, if I could get to sleep. I was so lost and confused. I didn't even understand why I was still so sad. I mean for all intents and purposes I was in my *element*…this was the prime time of my life! I graduated top of my class in both my undergrad and graduate school programs. I had an amazing support system in my parents, my brother, and my small network of close friends. I had an amazing job and a dedicated mentor who made herself available to me anytime. I seemingly had it all. But something inside of me wasn't settled and wouldn't let me be happy.

The last leg of my whirlwind vacation was spent in Cuba and the sights and sounds were simply delicious. On the final day, I was up super early and preparing to head to the airport. I felt a bit frazzled that morning because I hadn't really gotten much sleep. I felt like a zombie, moving slowly and not fully present. Even though I'd had breakfast at the resort I wasn't able to truly savor those final moments as much as I would have liked. I didn't want to leave though, so I was irritable. As I was heading down to the reception area of the resort to check out I didn't feel grounded, but I shook it off. I stood outside of the resort waiting for the Sprinter van that was taking me and several others to the airport.

It was hot, and I was annoyed because I wanted to have a car service all to myself. When the Sprinter pulled in, I felt someone's hand on my arm and turned quickly to see who was touching me. The touch agitated me. The person said, “I’m sorry, I just wanted to tell you that the color of your dress is very flattering on you.” I stood there awkwardly, peering at him over my sunglasses. Actually, because of the sun’s glare, all I could make out was his silhouette. He was tall though (at least 6’3), had a deep sensual voice, and smelled like … hell, I don’t know what the scent was but it was mesmerizing. Then he said, “Once again, I’m sorry. I didn’t mean any harm. But you’re beautiful. I don’t know how I haven’t seen or run into you on the resort before now. My loss.” Then he got onto the Sprinter. I just stood there, like a damn zombie.

When we arrived at the airport, I quickly made my way to the Security checkpoint and got corralled through the line like cattle on a farm as is always the case when you travel internationally. I was anxious, annoyed, and completely exhausted; I simply wanted to get home. For as glorious a time as it was to see the sights and experience the many cultures, foods, and people over these last many months, the most appealing thing to me now was to climb into my own bed and sleep for a few days. It's always funny to me how you seemingly need to rest *after* a vacation. But I needed to catch up on rest, to settle this *unsettledness* inside me. I just couldn't shake it.

Once I finally made it to my gate I sat down, put on my oversized sunglasses, began flipping through one of the many magazines I had in my bag, and put on headphones to quiet the busyness and noise of the airport. It was all too overstimulating, and I had to zone out to prepare for this long flight home. As much as I loved to travel, I always got super worked up before flying. My anxiety was on "20" and I needed to chill. I'd been sitting there flipping through the pages of the Vanity Fair magazine when someone walked past me and I instantly zapped out of my trance. Mmmmm, I thought to myself. I immediately looked up, peering over the top of my glasses again to see who it was. I recognized that scent and, strangely, my body tingled. It was the guy from the resort. This time, however, I got the whole picture in the frame and not just the silhouette. This man was FOINE a hell!!!! Do you hear me??? Tall, had medium brown skin tone, a beautiful smile, and was physically fit. I could tell this by the way the linen shirt and pants he wore clung loosely to his frame. He was standing at the ticket counter asking a question and I could not stop myself from staring. I was in another trance but this one was not zombie-like. He turned around and I clumsily dropped the magazine on the floor. I reached down to pick it up and he was there, stooping down in front of me. I looked up and all I saw were teeth. "*Hey stranger,*" he said, still smiling. "*You dropped something.*" I took the magazine from his hand but couldn't say anything because I was overwhelmed by his presence. He just took up space and it made me warm all over. I finally uttered, "*Thanks*" and I think I smiled. No, I'm sure I did. A big ass goofy smile but I couldn't help it. He said, "Have a safe flight" and walked away. I was so fucking hot from the inside out. Not temperature hot, this was horny hot. I quickly got up and went to the restroom to gather myself. "*Girl get yourself together... you acting like you've never seen a handsome man before, damn,*" I was uttering quietly to myself as I looked in the mirror and put on lip gloss. Then I giggled a little bit. This had been the first time I'd allowed myself to feel anything or have any type of reaction regarding men since the whole situation with Ty. Years had gone by, and I had been stuck there emotionally. This stranger reminded me of what it's like to *feel* again, even if on the most surface level. The attention he'd shown me felt nice. I wanted more of it; I deserved more of it. It was time and I was going to get out of my head and most importantly out of my way.

We boarded the flight; I found my seat and almost instantly fell asleep. I won't lie, while making my way to the seat I peered around coyly to see if the guy was on the same flight or perhaps was seated near me. I didn't see him though so I allowed myself to settle in and drift off. I'd slept for most of the flight and was awakened by the flight attendant announcing we would be landing soon. I got up to use the lavatory and as I was exiting, I stopped dead in my tracks.

There he was. He was in an aisle seat and appeared to be asleep. I was frozen, afraid for some reason to walk past him. The flight attendant was in the jump seat and asked if I was ok. I replied, "Oh yes, I'm fine, sorry." I slowly started walking towards him and had almost cleared getting past him when he grabbed my hand. I stopped and looked down at him. He pulled me towards him and whispered, "You following me?" His breath was warm and smelled sweet. I blushed and the tingling was back. In fact, everything was on FIRE. I slowly pulled my hand from his and replied, "Maybe… catch me if you can." Then I quickly made my way back to my seat. *"Girl WHAT????? Catch me if you can??!!* Lena Timmons, what in the entire world has gotten into you?!" I smiled for the duration of the flight. I was into this sexy little game with this stranger. And if for no other reason, it just brought me back to a sense of myself. The part of myself that made me feel attractive, wanted, and sexy. It woke something up in me that had lay dormant for the last few years. But honey the cookie was awake and in full working order. She was ready.

We deplaned and I made it through Customs and finally to the baggage claim area. I was still giddy from the exchange with the handsome stranger. But I was also exhausted and ready to get home. I pulled out my phone to call the car service. Then I heard his voice behind me. "You don't need to call me, I'm right behind you," he said. I smiled, finished the call, and turned to face him. "I'm Lena." He responded, "I'm Troy."

Troy and I hit it off right away. We didn't waste much time at all. We quickly learned what was important about each other; immediately covering topics like career, education, family, traumas, friendships, relationships, life goals, etc. The one thing, however, that drew us close and always brought us back to the "*center*" was our sexual connection. It was strong, it was intense, it was animalistic. From the moment we'd first encountered each other at that resort, there was an almost magnetic and sexual attraction that was undeniable. I found myself being all excited like a young schoolgirl. I'd even started doing shit like doodling my married name on scratch paper. *Mrs. Troy Bowers. Dr. Lena Timmons – Bowers. Mrs. L. Timmons-Bowers.* It had a bit of a ring to it, I thought. He had me all twisted up inside. The first time we got together intimately, he came by my place. We sat, kind of awkwardly in the beginning talking about random stuff. I'd asked why he was traveling alone and he came back to me with the same question. We talked about our family dynamics and had some things in common but there were aspects of our lives that were vastly different. I'd grown up in a two-parent, middle-class family structure. He'd come up in a household with a single mom who was not very maternal. He has siblings that were not very focused or productive in life. He was the only one in the family that had aspirations to do more and set clear goals for himself. His mother did not support him in any way, and he was deeply affected by that. I couldn't relate to that, coming from my experiences with my family, but I admired his tenacity and his unwavering loyalty to his family, despite it all. Even amid the chaos and calamity of his upbringing, he loved them. I felt like their lack of support and belief in him almost fueled him in a way that pushed him harder. There was something very compelling about that to me. We talked more that night, like hours more, and then he just grabbed me. He pulled me close to him and placed his mouth on mine, and I melted. He kissed me so slowly and softly that I felt like I wanted to cry. He started with my mouth, then my cheeks, my forehead, and my neck. I hadn't felt like this in a long time. But I also never *this way* before. Not ever. We were locked into this deep, soft, warm, and wet exchange for what felt like an eternity. Just repeated instances of soft moans and caressing. Then something shifted and he stood up, took off his shirt, and undid his pants. I followed suit and took off the sundress I was wearing. We were initially on the sofa but moved to the floor of my den. He pulled my panties off completely and began to kiss me. This time not on my mouth. He pleasured me in the most sensual, cautious, and attentive way. I had never felt anything like this in my life. His tongue was buried so deep inside me that I was squealing aloud; I could hear myself but couldn't stop. He seemed to take pleasure in that and was saying something to me, but I couldn't hear him. I called out to him "Please wait, please stop" because I was so overcome by the sensation of it all that I thought I'd peed on myself. He said, "You're ok baby." I said, "No, I think I peed." He responded, "Naw babe, that's all you. It's good. You taste so sweet." I was blown back. I didn't know how to process what was happening, but I wanted it. I wanted more. Troy took his time with me. He made sure he took great care to pleasure me. I'd look down at him and see the intention behind every motion he made. It was unreal. At one point I started trying to crawl away because the sensation was too much to bear but his arms were locked around my thighs and he kept pulling me back to him. I squealed so loud at one point and then screamed, "Troy, please wait!" He looked up at me, licked his lips, and climbed on top of me. His dick was so big and hard so when he entered me, I moaned so loudly I was sure my neighbors heard it. This man was ready for me and buried himself deep inside of me. He placed his body on top of mine and thrust himself in me with such a calculated rhythm that I felt like I'd left my body. It was surreal. "Who is this man?" I thought to myself. We howled and moaned like two animals in the wild. We made love in every way, for the next several hours, covering every inch of that room. It was hot, sweaty, funky, nasty and extraordinary. Troy awakened something in me that I didn't know existed. He taught me how to love and appreciate myself and my body. Every interaction with him was electric. Every. Single. Time. This had only been night number one. This was just the beginning.

Seven: **Fawning**

~seeking favor by servile flattery or exaggerated attention~

-7-

The first year with Troy had been pure bliss. I'd never had someone attend to me and my needs in the way that he had. He took great care to be certain I was satisfied sexually; he paid attention to fulfilling me emotionally and he worked hard to ensure I was gratified psychologically. He put it on me, and I was hooked. From the outside looking in, this was a relationship that anyone would marvel at and desire to have. All needs were being met, he was present and "all in", in all ways, all the time. It was amazing. At first. Often I had to pinch myself to be sure it was really real and acknowledge that I deserved this. I'd think about Momma and recall all the things that she tolerated from Dada. What would they be to each other and how would their relationship be today if he was "this" man to her? Would she have stayed if he were different? Why had she stayed given the way he was? That played out in my mind, constantly. And it began to affect how I viewed Troy. As amazing as he was to me, I was constantly waiting for the other shoe to drop. I almost wanted something bad to happen.

One Saturday afternoon, we were heading to an event for his company and I got what I'd been waiting for. Troy was in Sales, and it suited him. He was handsome, very charismatic, and could talk to anyone. It didn't matter where we were, he either knew someone or would strike up a random conversation with people. In the beginning, I was turned on by that. He had a way of pulling you in, in a hypnotic kind of way, when he engaged in conversation. That's what captivated me about him when we first met. The charisma, the charm. It was undeniable. But on this sunny afternoon car ride, I was not into it. So, as we drove to the event that day, I found myself a bit despondent. As we were driving he reached over and grabbed my hand. I quickly pulled away. He said, "Babe you good"? I didn't respond. "Babe, what's wrong"? he asked a bit more firmly. I still didn't respond. We drove for another 15 minutes, and he exited the expressway. He pulled over and put the car in

Park. "What's wrong with you"? he asked. I kept staring straight ahead. There was a long, awkward silence, and just as I was about to finally respond Troy said, "Lena get your shit together and you better not fucking embarrass me." I turned and looked at him, *What did he say? Who is he talking to?* I had a whole dialogue going on in my head and just as I opened my mouth to ask, he reached over the center console and grabbed my chin, firm and hard. He said, as he looked me square in my face, "Uh uh, don't say shit *now* Lena, just get yourself together." I had NEVER seen him behave in this way and he certainly had NEVER put his hands on me. Not like this. I complied and I didn't say a word. My jaws were throbbing and I wanted to pull the visor mirror down to look at my face but I was afraid. He put the car in Drive and we proceeded to our destination. Not one word was spoken, it was extremely unnerving.

When we arrived at the event, I spent the majority of the time drinking. Most of the time there for me was a blur. Troy toted me around on his arm like a doll and I remember smiling as we *worked the room*. A fake "hello" followed by an even faker "ha ha ha" is all I can recall about the night. The only other recollection I had was the painful grip Troy had on my hand. At one point, I almost teared up. I stepped away to go to the ladies' room and gather myself. One of the wives of his coworker was in there as well. We stood side by side in the mirror and smiled at one another. She was side eyeing me so I made a point to stand tall with quiet confidence as I adjusted my dress and touched up my makeup. She said, "Lena, right?" I nodded with a fake grin. She said, "Wow. Troy is a lucky man, you are stunning." I thought, "*Yeah bitch he is lucky. And who the fuck are you to comment on it anyway? What do you know about it*?" I mean, I knew he was one of the youngest members of the Executive team and there was likely a ton of scrutiny taking place for him. That's a lot of pressure for a young Black man to withstand. It made me think about how Dada worked hard to groom me and Lenny, telling us that we would always have to grind harder and stand firmer than anyone else.

Maybe this is why Troy was so aggressive with me in the car, I thought. Maybe he was nervous. I shouldn't lend to anything that makes him feel unseen or unheard. As his woman, I needed to do better. Stand by his side and make him feel confident at all times. Maybe if Momma had done this, Dada wouldn't have continually strayed. She needed to make him feel wanted. She needed to show him that he was appreciated. The woman in the restroom was still talking, but I was tuned out. I reapplied my lip gloss, offered a sly smile, and walked out to join my man. When I found Troy he was sitting at the table chatting with his colleagues. I sat next to him and gripped his thigh. He shot me a look and I removed my hand. *What did I do wrong? What was happening? Isn't this what I should be doing?*

We did not speak at all on the ride home. Instead, he turned on the radio and blasted the music so loudly that I had to close my eyes to try and zone out. My anxiety was at an all-time high. I was so confused, uncomfortable, and eerily afraid. When we pulled in front of my townhome he turned the music down, unlocked the doors, and said, "Get the fuck out of my car." I was stunned. In the year we had been together, I had never seen this side of Troy. I didn't know this person. I reached for the door handle and then stopped, turning to face him. "Troy," I said softly, "Please tell me what is happening right now." He had his head down and said something that I couldn't quite make out. So, I simply asked, "What did you say?" Before I could take the next breath, he backhanded me in my face. I shrieked and covered my face with my hands. He turned off the ignition and got out of the car. My door opened and he grabbed my arm. I still had my hands over my face and could now feel warm liquid oozing between my fingers. We got to the front door, he opened it, and we walked inside. I went straight to the bathroom and closed the door. I was afraid to pull my hands away from my face. *What just happened, is this real*? When I pulled my hands away, I could see my nose was bleeding and I had a small cut on the top lip. I turned on the faucet to run cold water and then began to cry. In fact, I sobbed. *How did I get here? What the fuck just happened? How did I allow this to happen?* I stood in the mirror tending to my wounds, and Troy knocked on the door. I didn't say anything. The door opened slowly. He walked over to me and said, "Baby, look what you made me do. You know I would never intentionally put my hands on you. I've never done this before, have I? But you forced me. You knew this was an important event for me. I can't have you shut down on me again. Ok? I'm sorry. It will never happen again." He tended to my wounds. He grabbed both sides of my face and kissed me. He then kissed me softly on my mouth. He continued to kiss me and I took it. I took it *all* in. Every bit of what he had given me, I took it. All of it.

We went into the bedroom, and he laid me down on the bed. I was still crying. Troy kissed my tears, licking them away at times, and then slowly began to take my clothes off. I think I was in shock, I'm sure I was. I didn't know what I was supposed to do so I let him soothe me. He knew how to do that without question. I just wanted this to all go away.

He started rubbing his face against mine from my forehead and worked his way down, all the way down. It felt warm and soft. I could smell his cologne and the faint scent of the champagne he'd had at the event was on his breath. Troy knew exactly what to do. It almost felt like some kind of sick game, but I played along. Before long I was naked, and he was inside of me. Stroking me slowly, with focused intention. He whispered, "Baby I'm sorry. Baby I love you. It's just you and me." And I cried. And I told him I loved him too. And I told him that I was sorry too.

It would be another six months before Troy would strike me again. We were at his friend's house for a barbeque. These were mostly his childhood friends and a few of his cousins. I had invited my friend Ava who I kept in touch with after college. She was the only person who knew about my history with Ty. We never lost touch with one another and despite all that she knew, she never mentioned it. I always loved her for that. It was good having someone that *I knew* there with me. Almost always at these events with

Troy, I felt like a fish out of water. I mean his friends were nice and I could seemingly get along with anyone, but I never felt fully comfortable. Ava came with her guy Marcus and they made such a handsome couple. She worked in the Communications field, and he was an Investment Banker. He reminded me of my Dada in some ways and, for that reason, it was easy to talk to him.

Troy and Marcus seemed to get along the whole day talking about sports and business and all that kind of thing. Ava and I were also having a good time, laughing, and making plans to connect and possibly travel throughout the summer. It felt really good. I hadn't felt this good in a long time. I'd look across the room from time to time to see Troy smiling at me and I'd get all tingly inside. This felt really, really good. Normal.

I was sitting down eating and Marcus sat down next to me. "Hey Lena, thanks for inviting us," he said. "Ava and I need to do this more; we get so bogged down with work sometimes that we forget to get out and have fun." I said, "Yeah I get it, Troy and I are the same." We chuckled a bit and talked more as I ate my food, he sipped on his cocktail and the music played in the background. This felt good. I excused myself to go to the restroom. As I walked into the house, Troy followed behind me. I turned to him and said, "You ready to go babe? I'm just gonna go tinkle." He smiled and put his hands on my hips pushing me towards the restroom. I giggled. *He's such a freak*, I thought to myself, but I was into it. When we got inside the bathroom, he closed the door behind him and before I could turn around he punched me in the back of my head. I fell forward into the sink, dazed. I held onto the sides of the sink to steady myself and then WHAM! He'd hit me again landing his hand firmly on the entire right side of my head. My ear was ringing. My eyes wouldn't focus. I held onto the sink and Troy bent me over, undid his pants, and entered me. Hard. He grabbed my hair in one hand and covered my mouth with the other. One single tear fell from my eyes as he whispered, "How dare you sit in my face and entertain another motherfucker. You wanna fuck him don't you? Is that what you want Lena? Now look what you've made me do." I'd heard this before. I did this. This was my fault. When he finished, he turned on the faucet and grabbed a decorative hand towel hanging near the sink. He wiped himself and then threw it at me telling me to get myself together. He stood there watching me as I looked at myself in the mirror. My eyes were red and the ringing in my ear wouldn't stop. He reached past me and grabbed a paper towel, wetting it. He placed it on my forehead and then opened the bathroom door with this arm around my waist guiding me out. We walked into the kitchen and Ava was standing there. "Hey, I've been looking for you Lena, you ok?" she asked. I wouldn't look at her directly, but she never dropped her gaze on me. Troy apologized saying that I'd gotten ill, and we needed to go home. Troy's family and friends were all staring and whispering. His cousin stepped up and said, "T, she a'ight?" Troy responded, "Yeah bro, she a lightweight. I'll holla at y'all later." Then

Ava asked again, “Lee, you ok?” I shook my head yes. Ava was not buying it. She was about to say something to Troy but Marcus stopped her. I looked up slightly, *as much as I could*, and gave a half-fake smile. “I’m ok, really, I just need to get home and lie down. Must have been something I ate. I’ll call you later girl.” As we walked past Ava she placed her hand softly on my back. I began to cry. No sound, just tears.

We said nothing on the way home. Troy walked me into the house and took me to the bedroom. In the same manner as the last time, he kissed and licked my tears, fucked me, and told me it would never happen again. He whispered, “Baby I’m sorry. Baby I love you. It’s just you and me.” And I continued to cry. And I told him I loved him too. And I told him that I was sorry too. I did this. This was my fault.

Eight: **Fractured**

~split or fragment so as to no longer function or exist~

-8-

I spent the next couple of years walking on eggshells in my relationship with Troy. I never knew what would trigger a reaction in him and found myself constantly trying to ingratiate him, always at my own expense. I didn't have many close friends besides Ava. She was my homegirl and we remained close through and beyond the college years, but she was worried about me. She was the one I could call for anything at any time. We would see each other several times a week and she became a tried and trusted support for me. I would continually invite her over to the house but began to notice a pattern in the number of declines. She didn't like Troy. She certainly didn't like Troy for me. Troy made her very uncomfortable, and Ava was the type of friend who had a slick tongue, meaning she would *tell it like it was* with no filter. That's what I loved about her. When we first met, she walked up to me in the campus bookstore and said, "Girl you bad bitch." I looked at her like "What?" and then she said, "That outfit is cute as hell, work that shit, sis." I was taken aback and a bit embarrassed because of how I initially was planning to respond to her bold statement. Being from Chicago, you find yourself ready to snap back at someone when they feel confident enough to say something slick or smart. But I'd come to love that boldness about Ava. She never changed and she never compromised herself for anyone. I truly admired that about her. She was also from Chicago and though we didn't meet until college, it felt like we'd known each other for our entire lives. Ava's personality was infectious and she was so damned funny. She was blunt, sometimes loud, always funny as hell, and loyal without question. No matter what, I knew I could depend on her. So, in this season of my life, her friendship meant the world to me.

Ava was that friend that I could call on for anything and vice versa. In college, she would always have some crazy shit going on with one of her guy friends and would rope my dumb ass into it. At any moment I could receive a call and hear her say, "*Bitch let's go, this nigga got me fucked up*," and I'd be in the car heading to pick her up. We'd go off galivanting to some area that we were unfamiliar with in Baltimore to chase down some knucklehead she was fooling around with. One time she called me in the middle of the night with some mess. "Lena, get the fuck up! This nigga got a bitch at his house. Lena, wake yo ass up!! We need to roll up on him and kick her ass!" Nuff said. If she was rocking,' I was rollin'. We hopped in my car in our PJs and drove smack dab into an area of Baltimore, where we did not belong, to confront the biggest thug of thugs and his side piece. One thing about Ava, she didn't give a shit about anything when it came to feeling played or disrespected. When you crossed her she was going to get in your face and tell you how much she didn't appreciate it. It didn't matter where, when, or how it went down. So, in this instance, while the disrespect occurred over the phone initially, Ava felt like she needed to take it straight to the source. And my dumb ass went along with it. We pulled up to this man's house and Ava jumped out of the car, screaming at the top of her lungs.

She yelled for the guy; I referred to him as *"ugly dude",* and the side piece to come outside. To be honest, I couldn't tell you his name if you offered me a million dollars. So now, I'm standing in the driveway with a bat in my hand ready for who knows what. I literally have no idea what I'd gotten myself into but I was down for my girl. Ava was HOT and almost inconsolable. She was screaming and banging on *ugly dude's* door and then she started banging her fist on his car. I was still standing there with a bat. Like an idiot. All of a sudden the porch light came on and this big dude emerged at the front door. I mean he was *UH-GUH-LEE*. He was short, and fat with big pink "soup cooler" lips as we used to call them when I was a kid. I almost burst into a raucous laugh but had to keep mean-mugging him and assume the position of the faithful friend. I had seen him around campus but I'm certain he wasn't a student at Morgan State. Knowing Ava, he was likely older than us. In her mind, she thought these older dudes could offer her more than a struggling college student could. Her logic wasn't completely incorrect, but it was the type of older dude she chose that caused these types of issues. The fools she chose were usually hard-core *gangster* types; running in the streets, selling drugs, driving tricked out cars and they always brought the drama. This was Ava's thing, for sure. The drama. I always wondered why she went for this profile of a guy. And they weren't all unattractive like him, but my girl's choices would sometimes stretch the limits of visual imagination. This was one of those times. As I stood there with a bat in hand, unsure of my fate, I was contemplating the importance of life's choices. The *ugly dude* stepped onto the porch with a joint hanging from his mouth and started yelling at Ava. "Bitch, you can't be serious right now! Why the fuck is you here and what old girl bouta do?" I guess I was *old girl*. I was in a firm stance with the bat squarely placed in front of me like some vigilante soldier awaiting the command of her chief. I was slowly peeing on myself, however, thinking *what in the entire fuck is happening here*? I actually think I said it aloud. He came down the steps of the porch and Ava was yelling at the fastest pace I'd ever heard. "*Nigga you got me fucked up! Tell that bitch to come outside! What's up? Yup, I'm here motherfucker! You know me, you know me, quit playing with me!*" I walked closer to Ava because he was getting closer to her as well. Now I was really afraid. This could go left, and quickly. Just as I was standing right behind Ava, *ugly dude* turned his gaze towards the door and the *side piece* was standing there. He screamed, "Gitcho dumb ass back inside, I told you to stay in the bedroom!" *Aw shit*, I thought to myself. That statement did it. Ava lunged at him and he grabbed her quickly, in a way that had her arms pinned to her sides. She was screaming, spitting, crying, and yelling, "Really nigga, that's how you gon' do me, and look at her white straggly ass!" Yes, the *side piece* was a white girl. I think that took it over the top for Ava. Nonetheless, and against my better judgment, I ran up to *ugly dude* and started swinging the bat like a crazy person. I mean, I couldn't let him manhandle her in that way. It almost set something off in me, it was like a trigger. I screamed, “Let her go motherfucker!!! Let her go!” I hit the side of his car and he yelled to someone behind me, “Get that bitch!” Before I could turn around someone grabbed me from behind, and I dropped the bat. I had no clue who had me subdued but it instantly sent me into what I now recognize was a panic attack. I felt like I’d blacked out for a minute because I was being held in a *bear hug-type* position, similar to how Ava was being held except it was from behind. I couldn’t calm myself and started flinging my head front and back trying to headbutt the person holding me but he was strong as fuck. I felt like I couldn’t breathe and started kicking my legs to try and connect with his shins. I was screaming and crying and felt like I was going to throw up. Suddenly, I felt a strange sensation come over me, like a quiet sense of calmness. At that moment, I realized that although my arms were pinned at my sides, my hands were free. I was able to twist my body and used my right hand to grab the nut sack of the person holding onto me. I grabbed his dick and balls and twisted, hard. He yelped, “Fuck!” and pushed me away. I almost lost my balance but I ran to Ava and started swinging on *ugly dude* with all my might. We were like two tornadoes throwing and landing blows on his ass from left and right. Ava spotted the white girl on the porch but she never came down the stairs. Instead, she had a cell phone in her hand and had called someone telling them she was being jumped. Raggedy, lying bitch. We were in the hood so the neighbors were too busy looking and laughing and couldn't care less about calling the police. We needed to get the fuck outta there. I looked over and realized that the person who had been holding me was this guy I'd seen in one of my classes. He apparently lived across the street from *ugly dude*. *Wow*, I thought to myself, in class he was nice to me, and we always spoke. But tonight, he crossed the fucking line. When I saw him holding onto himself wincing in pain, a small part of me felt sorry for him. But I just wanted to get the fuck out of there. Ava was still swinging at *ugly dude* and cussing him out when he finally said, "Ava quit fucking playing, just get the fuck out of here!" I agreed with him. I grabbed her arm and started pulling her to the car, picking the bat up along the way. We peeled out of there afraid the cops would be behind us, but they never came. Once we'd driven about 10 minutes or so, we were stopped at a light and I turned to look at her. She was looking straight ahead and I saw a tear fall from her eye. I reached over and held her hand. Despite the chaos, the potential of inflicting bodily harm and even going to jail, I was there for my friend. She knew that. She could trust that. And I knew that of her. I could also trust that.

Troy, of course, didn't like me hanging with Ava because I think he saw a side of me that he couldn't control when she was around. She brought something out in me that made him uneasy. So, he would intentionally do or say things that would make her uncomfortable when she came to our place. He would pick an unnecessary fight or behave in a way that would obviously affect my mood. Ava was always cool about it though. She would just sit back and wait to see how I would react. Almost wanting to say, "Bitch I know you ain't gone let him say this or do that to you." Sometimes I would get up the nerve to "*check him*" with the underlying fear of how and when he would retaliate against me. I just never trusted that I would be okay and more times than not, I wasn't. I became used to it, and almost expected that he was going to attack me, mentally or physically, anytime I'd hang out with Ava. He didn't want me to make any decisions without consulting him first. He didn't want me to go places that he didn't approve of. He didn't want me to work late without asking his permission. He didn't want my friends or family coming to our home without his knowledge and approval. If I took it upon myself to do anything without his input, I paid for it. For years to come, I would cover up the physical and emotional scars. I'd mastered it. My colleagues, friends, and some family members thought Troy was the perfect fit for me. We looked good together, indeed. We complimented each other. Everyone thought nothing but the best of us because we would smile and be completely tethered to each other in public but behind closed doors, we were severely fractured. And that's how we lived for a long time. Ava just couldn't sit and watch it any longer. She refused to see me in this way. She wanted to show up for me in the same way I had for her that night all those years ago with *ugly dude*. Nothing could stop us and we were there for one another no matter what. That's how we've always been. Right there, just one phone call away. Ride or die. But somehow Troy stepped in and affected our friendship in a way that seemed irreparable. I felt helpless. I knew what I *should* do, but I had some unwavering loyalty for him that slowly began to tug at the strings of the connection I'd had with Ava. We were coming apart. We tried over the next several years to try and stay connected through the shifts our lives took but it never felt the same. And that wasn't us. For Ava, not being able to see things come back to the center for us took a huge toll on our friendship, and she significantly cut back on visiting me. Over time, she cut back on answering my calls. We eventually stopped talking altogether. I was broken and damaged in so many ways. I tried to suppress this from everyone. For a while, it worked, until it didn't.

Soon the panic attacks got worse.

Nine: **Father**

~a man in relation to his child or children~

-9-

It had been some time since I'd seen my parents. With all that I had endured with Troy, it just became difficult to feign happiness and bliss for my immediate family. Lenny, my brother, was cool with Troy but always told me that he felt something was off with him. The situation with Ty really impacted Lenny. He wasn't innately an overprotective brother in the traditional sense so after the Ty situation he pulled himself away from my relationships. He wasn't fully aware of all that was happening in my relationship with Troy, by design. I only let him see and know what I wanted, and he never probed. It's not that he wouldn't have shown up for me, but I didn't let him in. He was always traveling with his job or booed up with some new *hottie* that he didn't have time for my shit. Not to mention Lenny had an extremely volatile temper. I knew that if had he known how things were really going down with me and Troy, it would not end quietly. I could not bear the thought of Lenny hurting someone and ending up in some fucked up situation. I would never forgive myself for that. I had this under control. So, whenever we spoke it was always based on what was happening in the immediate family. With the angst and drama at home, I would often escape to my parent's house as a kind of refuge. Troy wouldn't balk as much when I told him I was coming to see them. And in recent months, he straight up didn't seem to care. He was doing his own thing which left me wondering and worrying. Something was very off between us.

It was always good to be back home. Momma and Dada were still very busy with their careers and seemingly appeared to be happy. I marveled at their ability to be polished and poised. Sometimes I side-eyed it too. I mean, knowing that there was discord between them when we were younger I felt like I was watching and waiting for the *other shoe to drop*. Momma was always so warm and smelled good all the time. Each time I'd show up, she would give me the longest and tightest hug. "*Hey, my lovebug*," she always said. I could stay in her embrace for hours. She made me feel safe and seen. The anxiety in me would subside and I felt present and grounded. I could look right into my mother's eyes and lose myself in them. She just had a spirit of calmness and comfort that made you want to lay in the middle of the floor and tell it all. But I didn't. I couldn't. But I knew she could tell that something was off with me. I couldn't say the words out loud and tell her about all the terrible things that happened. Or the things that were happening. I just couldn't. So, we would sit sometimes and not say anything. I loved that because she knew that I needed the stillness. I needed to sit in silence and let her be the shield to protect me from all that we didn't say to one another. I almost felt like she needed this too. There was a silent storm inside Momma that was also brewing. I noticed it more when I visited the house these days. So, we sat there together. In the deafening silence.

Dada was not home most of the time when I visited. I knew he was busy; he had always been a guy on the go. I remember this from when I was younger and it carried through my young adult years. But it was interesting to me that he would still be on the go as much nowadays. Momma would say things like, "Girl, you know your Dada. He can't sit still for long. Something is always going on for him and he must tend to it right away." It's just that it was becoming more obvious how often he was away, and it was a lot lately. I'd mentioned it to Lenny and his response was, "Lena why do you care? Dada always runs the streets. This ain't new. And Momma isn't tripping, so why do you care?" I said, "I'm just saying, like damn they just don't seem to spend a lot of time together anymore. Momma has her friends and still does her running and shopping but when do they do things together?" Lenny told me I was being dramatic and to leave it alone. He said I can't just show up and make such broad statements about their relationship. But something felt weird to me despite his comment.

On this particular visit, Momma planned to cook up some food and throw some things on the grill. It was beautiful outside so we had the windows open letting the warm summer air flow in. Music was playing in the background and the smell of the lit charcoal was wafting into the house. Lenny left to run to the store and get ice and other things Momma added to her growing list. "Don't forget my wine, Lennox!" I smiled because Momma did not play about her wine, honey. I am the same way. I love a good bottle of wine. We were in the kitchen chopping up veggies for salad, singing Anita Baker songs, and prepping the steaks for the grill when I heard the front door open. I thought, *Dang that was quick. Lenny is back already?* But it was Dada. He walked into the kitchen and had the strangest expression on his face. I smiled but then asked, "What's wrong Dada?" He stood there for a moment as if he was struggling to respond. Then he said, "Hey Lena doll, so happy to see you." He grabbed me and hugged me so hard I had to catch my breath. I pulled away and asked, "What's wrong, you ok?' I looked him straight in the eye. His gaze made me feel different than Momma's. In this moment, I didn't feel safe; in fact, I felt a strong sense of discomfort and uncertainty. He stepped back from me and unconvincingly said, "Yes, Lena doll, I'm fine. Ya'll got it smelling good in here that's for damn sure. Where's Lennox?" He was deflecting. Momma responded to the question without even turning around and said that Lenny had run to the store. Dada had already started to walk out of the kitchen before she could finish her statement. I stood there thinking, *What the hell is happening here? Why are they acting so weird?* Meanwhile, Dada walked to the front of the house and began peering out the window like he was looking for or expecting someone to show up. Momma never turned around, she just kept chopping the vegetables. I followed Dada to the front room and stood close behind him. I peeked over his shoulder to see what he was staring at. There was someone in the driveway, next to Dada's car. The young man was just standing there and staring at the house. He was leaning on Dada's car as if he were waiting for someone. *Who is this person and why is Dada obviously so uncomfortable?* I cleared my throat so as not to startle Dada, but he knew I was there. Without turning around he said, "I thought you were helping your mother in the kitchen. You should go back and help her Lena." I heard something behind me and turned to see Momma standing there, wiping her hands on a dish towel. "Come Lena, we have to finish the salad and the steak needs to be turned." *What the hell is happening right now*, I thought in my head, *and who is the guy in the driveway*? Dada opened the front door and walked outside. I was about to ask Momma what was going on and she casually said, "That's his son." I started coughing and grabbed for the glass of water I'd been sipping on. "What did you say Momma?" I asked half choking on the water. "That is his son. That young man, in the driveway. He is your father's son." Momma slowly walked out the back door and went to the grill to turn the steaks.

I was in a state of shock. I was literally standing in the middle of the kitchen while. Momma was casually walking around as if she hadn't just said out loud what I knew I heard. She was acting as if she hadn't just dropped a nuclear bomb of information. I was stuck. Lenny finally came in and *whooshed* past me placing the bags on the counter. He asked, "Who is that outside with Dad? Dude looks familiar." Momma smiled and grabbed a pan before heading back outside to the grill and said, "Hmmm, I wonder where you may know him from? They say it's a small world, you know." I looked at her and tears started to well up in my eyes. *What the fuck is going on right now*, I thought. I turned towards Lenny and said, "Lenny. Momma just told me… I mean this guy is… Dada apparently…" but before I could finish my broken attempt to tell him what I had just learned from Momma, she put her hand on my arm. "Why are you crying Lena? Momma, what's up? Ya'll acting weird." Poor Lenny was confused and could sense something was really off. I finally sat down at the kitchen table and Momma stood by the sink with her hands on her hips. She took the bottle of wine from the bag Lenny brought in from the store and got three glasses from the cabinet. There was an eerie silence in the kitchen as she poured wine into the glasses. We were each about to take a sip of the wine when

Dada appeared in the doorway of the kitchen. "We toasting something?" he asked. I wiped my tears and saw Momma look at him with a glare that told me and Lenny that this was about to go left. "Momma, what's up? Who was the dude in the driveway?" Lenny asked again. Momma took a huge swig of her wine and said, "That young man is your….." Dada stopped her and said, "Wait Mo, wait, wait please just wait." Momma glared at Dada this time with tears in her eyes. Lenny stood up, "Momma, why you… What the fuck is going on?!" he shouted. "Sit down son, please," Dad asked softly. "No, somebody tell me, what the hell is going on!" Lenny said in a calmer but demanding tone. Dada sat down, hanging his head in tandem. He started to speak but the words wouldn't come out. He cleared his throat and started again. Momma leaned back onto the sink with another full glass of wine, glaring at Dada with a look of disgust on her face. I turned towards Dada and said, "Take your time." He started again, "The, uh, the young man in the driveway, is um, ...well his name is Jacob." Lenny blurted out, "Ok his name is Jacob and? Who is he? Damn! What is..." "He's my son!" Dada blurted. "Jacob is my son; Jacob is my son," he said, saying it a lot calmer and almost in a whisper. There was a long uncomfortable silence and then Lenny burst out laughing, I think he thought it was a joke. Momma was visibly annoyed and turned her back on us this time facing the sink. Lenny kept laughing with his hands covering his face. I got up quickly and walked over to tell him this was not the time to laugh but when I got closer, I realized that he was actually crying. He looked up at me and I felt helpless and extremely anxious. I'd never seen Lenny this way; his eyes told me all the things that his mouth could not. He grabbed at me and I fell into him. We didn't say a word. We just held each other and sobbed.

Dada sat with his head hanging low, looking only at the floor. He couldn't face us. Momma stood at the sink, her back to us. I stood up and said, "Someone, please, say something, PLEASE!" Momma never turned around toward us but said, "Tell them the truth Ray," and then she walked out the back door. Lenny got up to grab a paper towel. He cleaned his face and walked up to Dada. My heart was pounding out of my chest, and I felt like I couldn't catch my breath. I got hot all over and then I closed my eyes and took a deep breath in and then blew the air out. I did it again, *in breath, out breath, in breath, out breath, in breath, out breath*. Then I heard Lenny say, "Tell me. Tell us." *In breath, out breath, in breath, out breath, in breath, out breath*… now it was happening faster than before. I was really hot, and I could feel the sweat forming in my armpits and my hands were getting clammy. I balled up my fists to mask the dampness and tried to focus on my breathing… *In breath, out breath, in breath, out breath*… Dada started talking, I mean I could see his mouth moving but I couldn't hear anything. Lenny was standing face to face with him but I couldn't hear anything. I saw Lenny aggressively motioning towards Dada, like he was lunging and then I felt Momma brush past me quickly. *In breath, out breath, in breath, out breath*…. I tried to move towards them, to get to

Lenny, but my feet were glued to the floor. *In breath, out brea…..* The next thing I remember I was lying on the sofa. Momma said, "There she is, hey lovebug, you okay baby? Here take a sip of this." Momma handed me a glass of water. I looked around to gather myself and my surroundings. "What happened?" I asked. "You had a panic attack and passed out Lena. Are you having episodes again? I know today's news didn't help. I'm so sorry baby." We sat there for a time and said nothing. Then Momma put her head down slowly and softly sobbed.

Ten: **Fragile**

~not strong or sturdy; delicate and vulnerable~

-10-

It had been almost a month since the emotional *episode*. The events at my parents' house triggered one of the most significant panic attacks I'd had in a very long time. I'd ended up in the hospital for a few days after the disclosure of information about this secret *love child* my father had. Lenny was "MIA" and barely responded to calls from any of us. He'd only shown up at the hospital once and then simply disappeared. We were all struggling with this news, and no one talked about it since. But this is what we did. Anytime anything got real or heavy we stepped over it like something small that could be hidden and swept under the carpet. This situation, however, was like trying to step over a big ass boulder. There was no overlooking this one. But I didn't have the capacity to try to manage my own emotions let alone anyone else's. So I had to trust and believe that wherever Lenny was, he was okay. At least I prayed that he was.

From childhood, the experiences that I can recall didn't only affect me but Lenny as well. It was just different for us. I have vivid memories of significant and traumatizing physical and verbal abuse encounters between my parents. Memories flood my thoughts randomly and can even be triggered by certain sounds and even smells. The way our house smelled lives in me as an uncertain experience; especially in the moments when there was immense drama and sadness. The way my childhood blanket smelled is alive in me and can show up as an unfavorable sensation that I don't always have control of. Loud, raised voices in any form or circumstance and sudden noises can also trigger a visceral reaction in me. I might begin to sweat or feel a warm sensation come over me. Sometimes I lose my breath or feel like I'm drowning and get a ringing in my ears. Sometimes it's hard to swallow and at other times I feel compelled to run or escape, like I need to get out of the space that I'm in physically. It's as if I have no control over the emotion or feeling I am experiencing at the moment. I remember this happening to me a lot as a young child, but I had no idea why, when it would occur, or that it was something to be named, diagnosed, and treated. I'd never been one to invoke an argument because I don't like conflict. Verbal altercations result in a physical altercation, at least in my mind, or better yet, in my memories. So that's what I try to avoid. I carry those thoughts inside every day, and it's pushed down in a tidy little packaged compartment that sometimes comes undone. And when it does it shows up in me as behavior and action that says, *Let me find all the ways to make you happy and satisfy your needs so we don't end up in a space that we can't get out of or recover from.* When that doesn't happen, I come apart. Again, this has been my experience and coping mechanism. I realize it's not the healthiest and clearly doesn't always work out for me. But it's what I do, please others at the expense of mental and physical wellbeing.

Lenny's journey was a bit different. He didn't come up in the same timeframe as me and physical violence or abuse experiences were not as prevalent. Momma and Dada definitely had their *moments* but not in the same way as they had when I was little. Instead of physical violence, there was a lot of mental and emotional abuse taking place. For all of us. Dada was a "master" at manipulation and gaslighting. I hate to say that out loud but it's the truth. When I think back on some of the interactions that took place in our house and recall how things played out, it was Dada at that helm puppeteering exactly how he wanted things to go, to be perceived and to be understood. Period. And it didn't matter who was involved as long as the outcome suited his needs and purposes. This is what Lenny grew up seeing, experiencing and, ultimately, internalizing. As a man, with a father in the home, you ideally mimic and model the behavior that you see. Lenny watched Dada with big old puppy dog eyes, marveling at everything he did and everything he was. And he was *all that*. And he *knew* that. But we, his family, would also experience all the things he *was not*. The things he was not stood out more, at least to us; his wife, his children. Momma, of course, was on the receiving end of it. She knew the lover, friend, and life partner who was physically present but emotionally absent. He could show up and look good alongside her but couldn't connect with her on an emotional level, ever. He didn't have the capacity. I was the child on the receiving end of the memories of the man who lived down the hallway from me, with the loud voice, who beat my mother, who called her names, who said awful things about her. He didn't have a clue about the damage he had done to me. Lenny was the child on the receiving end of broken promises, demeaning commentary, and emotional distance. With all that, it's the love we each have for Dada that holds us hostage to him, despite his rage, his lies, his infidelities, his disappearing acts, and most importantly, his abuse. We somehow always found a way to move beyond it all.

I took a short leave of absence from work after this last emotional episode because I found myself to be really out of sorts. I was in a deep funk and not feeling good overall. Troy had been very distant from me before the situation at my parent's house, but he seemingly stepped up to support me. He stayed with me when I was admitted to the hospital and took me home when I was released. He cooked for me and tended to my every need. This was the Troy I fell in love with. We were spending more time together every day and he made sure that he was there to field off friends or colleagues that were incessantly trying to reach me. He sat with me when I broke down in tears and listened to me when I shared my thoughts on the situation with my parents. He offered his perspective on it all and even gave me some encouraging words about Lenny. He showed me that he cared, not just about me but about us. That truly mattered to me because it was a complete departure from how he had been behaving. He seemingly took care to notice that I was extremely vulnerable and fragile. And then something shifted.

One night, I was in the shower and Troy walked into the bathroom to ask how much longer I would be. I told him

I was washing my hair so it would be at least 10-15 minutes more. So, I suggested he get in with me. "Come in with me bae…" He didn't respond. "Troy, come get in with me while the water is still hot!" He still didn't respond. I finished up, rinsed off and got out of the shower. I walked into the bedroom and Troy was sitting on the bed. "Babe, you didn't hear me calling you? I wanted you to get in with me." He turned around and said, "Take off that towel." I laughed, "Troy please, I can't right now. I'm not in the right head space." He walked over to me and said, "Lena, you need this baby." He was probably right, but I didn't feel sexy or sexual. The last thing I wanted to do was be physically intimate, but Troy had been so attentive to me. In my mind, I thought, *How could he not know that now wasn't the time for this,* but I convinced myself that even in this fragile state I was in, I owed this to him. Next thing I knew, he'd reached underneath the towel and buried his fingers inside me with his mouth suckling the back of my neck. I let out a long, slow moan of ecstasy. *Shit, maybe I do need this*, I thought to myself. With his other hand, he pulled the towel away and grabbed me around the waist. His dick was hard as a rock and if I'm being honest, I don't remember the last time we'd had sex. He bent me forward on the bed and quickly undid his belt buckle and pants. He'd pulled his fingers from me, lubricating my cookie with my own juices, and then licked his fingers. I was so turned on by all this. It had truly been a long time since we fucked and I had forgotten how good this man was at this. Troy entered me from behind slow but deep. I held my breath as he stroked in and out and in and out and in and out. I was counting the strokes as I took in every inch of him. He pulled out quickly, put his fingers inside me again, and then put them in my mouth. He always did this. He said he wanted me to taste how sweet I was. I didn't mind. I loved everything about it. He then lifted me by my thighs so I was backward straddling him, this position resulted in a thrust so deep inside me that I screamed. But I wasn't in pain, at all. I was in the deepest zone of pleasure I had been in in a very long time. After he worked me for what seemed like an hour, he gently turned me around so that now I was on my back. He entered me from this position while lifting my butt off the bed, again, burying himself deeply inside me. My legs were wrapped around him, and he was holding me by the hips. Troy was the type of lover who looked you straight in the eye. For me, it was an intense turn on but when I shared this with my friends, they said it was weird and a bit egotistical on his part. I loved that he wanted to see my reactions and facial expressions. I wanted, hell I needed, that connection with my man. That's what it felt like, a connection between two lovers. Troy and I wore that bed out. He'd flipped me and folded me and licked me and rubbed me and sucked me and loved on me. I didn't realize until we were lying next to each other how much I needed this. It was a release that brought about a sense of calm in me. I slept like a baby that night, in the arms of my man. Happy, content, and connected. It would not last.

Eleven: **Fool**

~trick or deceive (someone); dupe~

-11-

Troy and I spent the next six months in what I would call *uncertain bliss.* What I mean by that is while the rekindling of our love journey felt amazing there was something about it that felt as if it were under attack. Nonetheless, we were moving forward, together. He hadn't shown any signs of the abuse that he had in the years prior and he made me feel like I had nothing to worry about. Troy had reestablished himself in his career and was on a professional high. I was happy to be by his side and happier to support everything about him. We attended dinners and business outings often. I became fast friends with his friends and their wives. Everyone was kind and seemed to support Troy as the strong, successful businessman he was. In some ways, it reminded me of Momma and Dada, which scared me because of their history and the other revelations. But I didn't want to compare our relationships. After all, Troy and I weren't them. We moved differently and this was a different time. The things Momma tolerated from Dada are not the same things I tolerated. I was stronger than that and if anything like that happened to me, I would leave. Well, I mean yes, he'd hit me once or twice but that was just out of frustration. He apologized for it, and it hadn't happened in months. So, we were good; we were different. Momma sustained far worse. I would leave if things got that bad. Period. And it goes without saying that if a kid came into the equation, I would end it. Period. I would definitely end it.

Like Troy, my career was coming back to life, and I was getting myself back on track. Amidst all the personal chaos of the last several years, I'd personally accomplished a lot. It just felt like a haze. I completed my degree earning my Psy.D. in Clinical Behavioral Psychology several years back and now I was working at the agency as a practicing Psychiatrist, seeing patients regularly. The additional success of obtaining my Ph.D. in Behavior Analysis catapulted my career in such an amazing way that Dr. Moore was thrilled to have me back. She was always the "other mother" to me, and thrilled or not, she cautioned me to take my time when I returned. She was simply amazing, and I felt so blessed and fortunate to work alongside her. I found my rhythm very quickly and we were becoming known as the premier Child, Adolescent & Adult Psychiatric agency in Chicago; owned and operated by an African American female clinician with an all-African American staff. Dr. Moore and I had begun some preliminary discussions around my taking part ownership in the agency to establish a regular client base. This is the type of situation you work towards as a psychiatrist, and I was feeling strong and ready to pursue it. I had dreamed of starting my own practice that focused on a number of emotional, behavioral and psychiatric disorders in young children. There were so many issues that were prevalent for this population, and I wanted to focus on the African American community specifically. Our children suffer from a wide range of issues like mood disorders, anxiety, neurodevelopmental disorders (such as attention deficit hyperactivity disorder and autism spectrum disorders), behavioral problems, and eating disorders which often go undiagnosed. The stigma in our community hinders the ability for clinicians to assess and diagnose our babies appropriately and they suffer for it. I wanted to affect change in this area. I was so passionate about it, and I think Dr. Moore could see it in my eyes. She took time to mentor and advise me along my path, so to be able to work with her was almost surreal for me. She worried about me and assured me that there was no need to rush this next step, but we agreed to work together on a strategy to move things forward in a focused and methodological way. It was an exciting time all the way around and I was basking in the glow of love and blooming success. What an amazing time it was for me. I was 32 years young, in love, and successful. Things just couldn't get better than that.

I was in my office one afternoon reviewing case notes and my administrative assistant, Nadia, stopped in. "Dr. Timmons, are you taking new clients right now? There is a young lady who said she was referred to you and wants to get on your calendar. Can I get her in?" I had been intentional about not taking any new clients since I'd been back to work. I wanted to gradually build myself back up to a comfortable client case load but something about the idea of a new client felt right. So, I agreed to take on this new client. "What's the name of the client, Nadia, and what is her age? Also, did you complete the initial assessment over the phone?" Nadia said, "Hang on a sec Dr. Timmons, let me get her information. Okay, her name is Mica Wilkins, and she is 5 years old. Yes, I got the assessment, well kind of, I attempted to complete it over the phone but the mother insisted she speak with you in person. Oh, and the mother's name is Erica." I replied, "Hmmm, ok. You said she was a referral. Did she indicate who told her about me?" Nadia shook her head "*no*" and shrugged her shoulders. *Interesting,* I thought. "OK, get her scheduled with me for this Thursday afternoon at 3p. Thanks, Nadia." I started to create a case file and wrote down *Mica Wilkins, age 5.*

Thursday turned out to be a busy, and rather hectic day for me. I'd had back-to-back clients all morning and a short lunch break where I attempted to level set. I'd learned in therapy to take small, intentional breaks for meditation and an opportunity to ground myself. I went into one of the client spaces, turned the lights off, and laid back on the sofa. I closed my eyes and set a timer on my phone for 20 minutes. I was super tired today, almost sluggish. I'd been feeling a little run down the last few weeks but attributed it to returning to a full work schedule. I had a doctor's appointment a few days ago and they did blood work along with a full physical just to be sure all was ok. And today had been crazy busy so that only reinforced the tiredness. It felt good to be still for the moment, so I sat in silence, taking deep calculated breaths. That is the trick… the breath and doing breathwork. When you master breathing, it enhances your awareness, deeply relaxes you, and improves focus. That's what I needed, focus. Today of all days, I needed to focus, more than I realized. This was one of the busiest days I'd had since coming back full time and I was feeling a bit overwhelmed. *Focus Lena, focus on the breath.* I'd learned so much about breathwork in my therapy sessions that I'd incorporate the importance of it to my clients, if it was appropriate for their diagnosis and treatment plan. I'd explain to them the meaning of breathwork, "Breathwork *refers to any breathing exercise or technique. People often perform them to improve mental, physical, and spiritual well-being. During breathwork, you intentionally change your breathing pattern.* Oftentimes, for my teenage clients, I'm sure most of what I said sounded like a character from Charlie Brown…" *wah, wah, wah, wah, wah, wah, wah, wah.*" But when I spoke to them about breathwork, something seemed to *click* and they were interested. Especially when I shared that it was a tool I used and personally put into practice. It made me relatable to them. This is one of the joys of doing what I do. I was making an impact. *Focus on the breath, Lena.* I knew my timer would go off soon, so I had to reset and take in these last few moments of stillness and quiet. *Breathe in, breathe out, breathe in, breathe out Lena.*

I had gone back into work mode and had about 30 minutes before the 3 pm appointment with my new client Mica Wilkins. I was finishing up client case notes when my phone rang. "Hello, this is Dr. Timmons." There was silence. "Hello??" I said again. Silence. I was about to hang up and when I heard, "Oh, I'm so sorry. I'd accidentally hit the mute button, is this Lena Timmons?" the woman asked. I answered, "Yes, this is Lena, who is this?" "Hi, I'm Diane, a nurse calling from Dr. Jeffries office. You'd come in last week for some blood work and he'd asked me to give you a call." My heart started racing a bit. "Ok, is everything alright?" I responded with a fake chuckle. The nurse said, "Yes, ma'am, everything is fine. Dr. Jeffries wanted me to reach out to let you know that the blood workup was good. All your levels are in the normal range. Kidney function is fine, and cholesterol level is fine. He also wanted me to let you know that he recommends the following OB/GYN doctors; *Dr. Sarah McKaegly, Dr. Rene Johansson, Dr. Beatrice…..*" I stopped her mid-sentence. "Wait. What do you mean OB/GYN doctors? I didn't ask for any recommendations. Why would I need an OB/GYN referral?" She paused and then said, "I, um, assumed you and he had discussed this since you're about 6 weeks along in your pregnancy Dr. Timmons". I put the breathwork into immediate practice. *Breathe in, breathe out, breathe in, breathe out Lena.* What the fuck, I thought to myself after hanging up the phone with Nurse Diane.

Nadia walked into my office to let me know that 3 pm had arrived. I'd been sitting at my desk staring out the window since speaking with the nurse from Dr. Jeffries' office. I was warm all over and now felt a bit nauseous. What the fuck? This cannot be happening right now. Troy and I had talked about having children at some point in our relationship. I mean, it's not like we didn't want kids or anything and we certainly knew the clock was ticking but we still had things we wanted to accomplish over the next few years. A baby? A baby. Wow. Maybe it's not so unheard of. I mean I am in my prime, I'm feeling good, Troy and I are in the best place we've been in in a very long time. A baby may just be the thing we need in our lives right now to bring it all together. To bring us all together. Things were still a bit fractured between me, Lenny, Momma and Dada since the "big reveal" but a brand-new baby would certainly bring much-needed joy into our lives. I continued pondering on the idea when Nadia walked into my office again, "Dr. Timmons, they're waiting for you."

I looked at myself in the mirror and touched my belly which made me smile shyly. *A baby*, I thought. Wait until I get home tonight and tell Troy. I adjusted myself and headed into the client's room. When I walked in, I saw the prettiest little girl sitting on the sofa next to whom I assumed to be her mother. The little girl was dressed in a pink sweatsuit with matching pink and white sneakers. Her hair was in three ponytails, one at the top and two at the back. My mom used to style my hair this way. She had long jet black, thick hair with little wispy baby hairs framing her chocolate-complected face. She was so pretty. Seeing her made me think about my baby. In fact, this little girl could easily be mine and Ty's. She kinda looked like him. I announced myself, "Well hello there Mica, my name is Dr. Timmons, or you can call me Dr. Lena." Mica looked up with her big beautiful dark brown eyes and gave me a cautious smile. I held out my hand to grab hers and we gave each other a quick handshake. I smiled and turned towards her mother. "Hi there, I assume you're Ms. Erica?" Mica's mother, Erica, smiled in a sly kind of way and acknowledged. "Yes, I'm her mother. I'm Erica." Her tone was weird, but I glazed past it. I was still a bit off-kilter from the earlier phone conversation. We also shook hands, and I sat on a nearby chair and asked Erica some preliminary questions. "So, I heard you were referred to me. May I ask by whom? What brings us together today? How can I help?" I smiled at Mica and then at her mom. Erica looked at me and again smiled back but it was a strange, almost devious smile. It made me feel uncomfortable and I started to feel warm. *Breathe in, breathe out, breathe in, breathe out*. She leaned over to Mica and whispered, “Mommy wants you to go with the nice lady in the hallway and wait for me, baby.” I was confused. “Um, isn’t this appointment for the child? I don’t typically see adults. I’m a Child Psychiatrist, Ms. Erica. I would be more than happy to refer you …” but before I could continue, she held her hand up as if to gesture “*Wait*.” Nadia appeared at the door and Mica held her hand out. Nadia escorted her into the hallway and closed the door. Erica walked back to the sofa and sat down. I was totally and utterly confused. “Um, ok. How can I help you, Ms. Erica?,” I said in an obviously annoyed but still professional tone. I adjusted myself in the chair and cleared my throat. I was feeling warmer now and a bit fidgety. *Breathe in Lena. Breathe out Lena.* Erica spoke. Erica spoke a lot. Most of what she said sounded as if I were listening through a drinking glass pressed up against a wall. I could make out some of the words but a lot of it was muffled. At times she was visibly angry, at other times she was sobbing uncontrollably. The entirety of the conversation was one-sided. Her side only. I didn’t say a word. I couldn’t move. I couldn't breathe. I sat and took it in. All the while telling myself to *breathe in, breathe out.*

Erica's dramatic monologue, recapped:

Hello Lena. I can't believe I'm finally sitting here with you, face to face. I'm sure you don't know me. I guarantee it. But I know you. Rather, I've known of you for a long time. We actually go way back, Miss Lena. I've been hiding in plain sight.

What is this woman talking about and who the hell is she? She is not familiar at all. I wanted Nadia to walk back into the office and interrupt, but this was my last appointment for the day. So, there was no need for her to come in unless I'd called for her. What is happening right now, I thought.

At the onset, when you could have known or met me, we ran in different circles. We were young. We were doing our own things, but we knew mutual people, well actually, one mutual person.

She paused for a long period of time. Looking directly at me.

> *Do you want to guess who our mutual friend is?*
>
> There was a long, dramatic pause. *No worries, I'll tell you. It's Ty. Ty Walters.*

She paused again, almost as if she were waiting for me to do or say something. But I could not move.

> *Yup, my baby, Ty. You both went to Morgan State University. But you left your Sophomore year and came back to Chicago to finish up at Loyola. You graduated in the top percentile of your class, which is amazing to me given all that you endured. Ty almost didn't graduate. Did you know that? He almost lost everything. Did you realize that? He was set up to fail and things got really bad for him, and it was all because of you. Did you ever think about that?*

I said, almost choking back tears, "That is not what happened. At all. Listen, I don't know what this is about, why you're here and I certainly don't know you. Please leave. Get out of my office now." She laughed. Hard. And she kept talking.

Oh no, love, I'm not going anywhere until I break it all down to you. This started with Ty, my first, one and only love, but it will end with you. I need you to understand what happens when you play with the wrong people, they will retaliate and then sit back to watch as things come apart. You almost ruined his life. And you certainly ruined our relationship. I've loved Ty since high school, and we were together all through college. I knew about you; he told me how he felt sorry for you because your friends had told him back in high school that you hadn't really been with anybody, and they dared him to get with you. He dicked you down and you were hooked, then he couldn't shake you. I don't blame you; Ty was a BEAST (she laughed). We were young and I was having fun too, so in the beginning I didn't care. He was getting it in with you and I was getting it in with him too, and others. I just didn't expect that this thing with y'all would carry on through college. He actually started catching real feelings for you and I was pissed.

My mouth fell open. I could not believe what I was hearing. Now, I was getting hot all over my body, literally from my head to my toes. I could feel my hands getting clammy and my feet, underarms, and under-boob were all damp from the anxious sweat. I wanted to come out of my clothes, right there in the office. My throat felt like it was closing, and I began to gag a little. *Breathe in, breathe out, breathe in, breathe out.* I reached over for the glass of water I had sitting at the side table. My hands were shaking uncontrollably. I almost wanted to close my eyes for a few minutes and open them again. *This had to be a nightmare.* I took a small sip of the water, spilling some of it on my lap. I pulled a Kleenex from the box on the table to dab at it. She was unfazed and she kept on talking.

I told him to break it off with you and he kept saying, 'She's so fragile and now her family is all into it, I just can't be cold like that.' I told him that I would confront you on campus and tell you about me and him. I'd make a big scene and then that would be it but he shot that down too. He caught feelings for you Miss Lena. But I couldn't have that now could I? I had to bring a screeching halt to it all. By any means necessary.

I ran over to the trash can just in time to throw up. She sat and watched me, smiling the whole time. I wiped my mouth and took another sip of water. Now I was pissed. I walked back to my chair, sitting on the edge, leaning forward, and staring at her eye to eye. "What the fuck is this about? What did you come here for? To tell me this??!! All this shit you're talking about happened years ago. Life has gone on for me, seemingly for us all. I have no idea what Ty is doing, nor do I care! He could be a fucking crackhead selling *M&M's* on the L for all I know. I don't give a shit. I suffered immensely at the hands of that man and don't want any parts of him. So now what? You got a strong reaction from me. Satisfied? Now I'll say it again, get the fuck out of my office." I was visibly furious at this point. I hadn't been this angry in a very long time. She could see it. I could feel it. *Breathe in, breathe out, breathe in, breathe out.* But instead of getting up to leave Erica leaned back on the sofa, crossed her legs, and smiled.

> *Um, yeah so, I'm not done Miss Lena. As I stated, I've loved Ty since high school. Our families were close, and it was like he and I were destined to be together. Allowing him to play the game with you in high school was only supposed to be that, a game. Somehow, shit shifted, and he got sucked in. No one could have predicted that it would have gone on for as long as it did. Not me, not him, no one. But it had to be shut down.*

Now she leaned forward. Looking at me square in my eyes. I felt like I was going to throw up again, but I held it in. I scooted back into my chair; I could tell that I would need something strong and sturdy to support me through what was about to come out of her mouth.

> *The infamous photo scandal back at Morgan State... yeah, so, I set it all up Miss Lena. I was the mastermind. With the encouragement and support of Miss Tiffany, I made it happen. Yeah, Miss Tiffany never, ever liked you. She was down for whatever it would take to break y'all up. So, she left it up to me and Ty just went along for the ride. Anything involving a good fuck, he was down with. It's the freak in him. So, going to the golf course, taking the photos, hell, even the photographer was all orchestrated by me. Shit, the photographer is my cousin. Ty told him about your aftergame ritual, and he followed y'all, every single time. Then we'd look at the pictures together; me and Ty. The problem was*

that Ty's dumb ass started sharing them with folks and that goof-ass dude from the band happened to be the boyfriend of your friend. It just spiraled out of control by that point. It was just supposed to be something that would break y'all up, not almost ruin him. But Miss Tiffany was on it, she got with Administration and shut it down. You choosing to leave Morgan State and going back to Chicago was a bonus. Ty and I were able to regroup over time and it was all good. Until it wasn't. I thought once you were out of the picture we would marry and ride off into the sunset. But that didn't happen. He never stopped loving you. He never stopped talking about you. He never stopped feeling guilty for hurting you.

She sat up straight and started to cry. So did I. But we were undoubtedly crying for different reasons. She kept talking.

I was broken. I was angry. We stopped talking altogether after college and ultimately, we lost touch.

How could he leave me? I'd been with him, held him down, and supported him in ways you never could. I couldn't understand it. I started following you on social media and kept in contact with people who knew you. I wanted to confront you and tell you everything. I thought that would bring me satisfaction, to see the expression on your face when you learned that I was Ty's woman and I broke you two up. But then that wasn't enough for me. I wanted you to feel the pain that I felt. I wanted you to feel what it feels like to be betrayed.

"What are you talking about? I did feel it. I lived it. I still live it. I suffer from anxiety and panic attacks as a result of it. That will probably never change. For as long ago as that was, I still feel it every goddamn day. It still lives in me. So don't fucking tell me about pain and betrayal. I know what the fuck that feels like, every time I lose myself to a panic or anxiety attack. And I have still managed to move on with my life. I don't give a shit about you or Ty. Fuck both of you!" She wiped her tears away and started laughing.

> *Miss Lena, Miss Lena, Miss Lena… please let me finish. Betrayal, pain, and revenge can come into our lives hard like a ton of bricks, or fast like in sweeping waves of water. In either case, it knocks the wind out of you and shakes you off your square. I always assumed that's what you felt with the whole photo scandal but in my mind that didn't match up to what I felt when Ty left me. And I'm sorry love, but you will have to pay for that. Soooooooooo, I've been watching you. In plain sight. We've crossed paths here and there as you have navigated your life. You've done some amazing things girlie. Bravo. I know so much about you, your family, your work. I know where you live. I know where you've been. I even know who you lay your head next to at night. He smells good, don't he? I know you like that cologne he wears. It's the same kind he wore when you met in*

Cuba. Mmmmm, yeah, he smells good. Fucks real good too. Been fucking me real good for years now. You call him Troy. Mica and I call him Daddy.

She got up to walk out of the office but left something on my desk. I tried to stand up, but my legs were too weak. I reached over to grab the glass of water on the table and knocked it over, breaking it. Nadia peeked inside to ask if everything was okay, I looked up at her, threw up on myself and passed out.

Twelve: **Fury**

~wild or violent anger~

-12-

Nadia cleaned me up and called Troy and he showed up to take me home. He came into the office with a serious but strained look on his face. I'd wondered if the bitch had already called him. He thanked Nadia and we walked outside. He got me to the car, buckled me in and walked around to the driver's side. When he got in, he asked me what happened and I simply said, "Ask Erica." He sat there for a few minutes staring straight ahead with a blank expression on his face. I continued, "Yeah, Erica came to my office under the guise of being a parent of a potential client. And she brought your daughter. Her name is Mica, right? Pretty little girl. I feel sorry for her. Her parents are two sick ass individuals. Sick as fuck, in fact. He took his hands off the steering wheel, clasped them together, and turned to say something, but I stopped him. "Don't say a motherfucking word. Not one. I cannot even begin to articulate how fucking disgusted I feel. How humiliated I am. How goddamn angry I am. You got me all the way fucked up Troy. I have lost myself in you, lost myself for you. And what have you done? Lied to me. Beat on me. Cheat on me. Use me. Fuck me. Literally and figuratively. Yeah, you got me fucked up. But you just wait. Take me home." He started the car, and he did just that. When we got home, I went straight into our bedroom, locked myself inside, and refused to see or speak to anyone for 2 days. Troy stayed home and tried to coax me out of the bedroom with pleas for forgiveness and cries of deep gut-wrenching sorrow. I didn't say a word. What was there to say? I needed him to leave but he would not. He told me he would prove that he was a better man than this no matter how long it took. Momma, Dada, and Lenny came by, but I wouldn't talk to them either or come out of my room. I could hear them yelling at Troy. Lenny was furious and screaming all kinds of hateful things. Momma was trying to calm him down and I heard Dada say. "Lena, we'll be back baby. We'll be back. But just say something baby, please." I couldn't take it any longer so I texted them all and said I had some things to work through and to trust that I would reach out to them when I needed to.

When Dr. Moore reached out a few days later, she told me that she knew I'd taken on too much too soon. She encouraged me to take a couple of weeks off to rest, reset, and gather myself. She assured me that my clients would be taken care of and that Nadia would rearrange or reschedule my appointments. I agreed because I absolutely needed time to sort out what had transpired.

By the end of the week, I was up and moving about the house like a crazy person. I was anxious, restless, irritated, and visibly angry, banging things around in the cabinets, throwing things, stomping through the house, clanging pots, and slamming doors. I felt like I wanted to destroy something. I contemplated bleaching all his clothes, but I stopped myself from doing it. What the fuck? Who am I right now? I was also nauseous, but I wasn't sure if it was the pregnancy or my nerves. When I get nervous energy like this and feel my anxiety peaking, I tend to want to cook or clean. So, I started doing both. I baked banana bread, and I chopped vegetables. I cleaned the entire kitchen including the refrigerator, stove, and pantry, rearranged the living and dining rooms, and cleaned the air vents and baseboards from top to bottom. Anything of Troy's I came across went into a pile that was slowly taking up residency in the guest bedroom. He'd been sleeping there since this all went down. I threw his shit in the room as I plowed through the house. I heard several things break as they landed. I didn't give a shit. I was so angry. There would be moments were I'd stop and look around our house and then burst into tears. How is this my life right now? Anything of his made me gag. At one point, I threw up in his bathroom and left the evidence in his toilet. I hated him and I wanted to hurt him. Shoot him in the balls, cut his dick off, beat him in the face until he was unrecognizable. I chuckled a little bit at some of the gruesome thoughts I had. *Now you sound crazy heffa*, I said to myself under my breath. I just wanted to show him as much of the hate I felt for him as possible.

I put up with so much in this relationship, most of which I had never shared with anyone, not even Ava. She was right about Troy all along. Right about the fact that I deserved better and that he meant me no good, from the beginning. I just didn't want to believe it, though I was living in it. She could tell the whole time. Troy was charismatic, handsome, and a master manipulator; all of which attracted me to him. I was sucked right into his swagger and fed on all the shit he spewed out of his mouth. And along with all that I put up with the lies. Oh yeah, and the women. And the women. And also, the women. I allowed myself to be degraded time and time again, allowing him to convince me that everything between us was fine. I would, from time to time, have friends and family tell me they saw him out in public with other women. Once he went to a pro basketball game and several of my cousins were there. My cousin called me from the game and said, "Hey cuz, where are you?" I replied, "Hey girl, I'm at home. What's going on?" She paused, and I could hear that it was really noisy wherever she was. She finally said, "Ummmm so I'm at the Bulls game tonight and I see Troy." She paused again. "Yeah, he told me he was going to the game. Did y'all speak?" I asked. "Um, no. He's with someone Lena." I felt my heart sink. I said, "OK. Um, did he see you?" "Yeah, he saw me. He saw us all. I'm with Javina, Braylan, and Missy." My cousin was pissed. I could hear it in her voice. Then she said, "What do you want me to do babe?" I said, "Speak to him. Let him see you." She said, "OK babe. Are you good? I'm sorry Lena. I'm not trying to be messy, but this is clearly not a friend he's with. This is..." I stopped her. "Yeah, I get it. And no worries cuz. Good looking out." We hung up the phone. I sat there feeling like I was about to vomit and cry. I closed my eyes to calm myself. *Breathe in, breathe out, breathe in, breathe out.* Within minutes, Troy was calling. I let the phone ring several times before answering. "Yeah, hey what's up," I said. He responded, "Hey babe, I just saw your cousins at the game. I spoke but they didn't say anything. Not sure they saw me." The audacity of the nigga, trying to feel me out. "Yeah, they saw you. I just spoke to Joi. She called me. Who are you with Troy?" He said, "Babe it's hard to hear you. Um, but I'm with some folks from the office." I chuckled. "Oh, so you're with several people? Joi said she saw you with a female. Who is it?" He said, "Huh? A female, oh that's just one of the chicks from the office. I tried to introduce her to Joi and them but by the time I made it to the area where they were standing, they had already gone." He was lying. Straight up lying. Joi would never have called me if it wasn't what it appeared to be, and I knew that. Troy knew that. But Troy also knew he'd be able to finesse his way out of it. And he did.

Then there was the time when one of his women was bold enough to call me. She told me she was in love and couldn't understand why he would be treating her the way he had because according to her, he said we were no longer together. I remember looking at my phone like, "*Girl, are you serious right now*." This woman told me far too much information about herself, her career, where she lived, what they did together, and how long the relationship had been going on. I was fascinated that someone could be this damn stupid. She told me that he would meet her at the movies but that she had to arrive before him and sit in the back of the theater. She gave him the keys to her house and car. She bought him all kinds of expensive shit, most of which I benefitted from. I found myself coaching and counseling her on building up her self-esteem and not allowing a man to take advantage of her in this way. I told her to have more self-worth. These are the things *I told her*. And then we even went as far as to trick Troy into meeting somewhere and when he arrived we were both there. He turned tail and ran like a little bitch. I told her to get her shit together and move on. I also told her not to call me or him again. And when he got home late that night, I was waiting for him in bed. I yelled. I screamed. I cried. He finessed me. He fucked the shit out of me. And I forgave him.

There were so many other instances of his infidelity and breaches of my trust. Numerous opportunities for me to walk away, scot-free. He would dig his own grave and I would be there to help him fill the dirt back into the hole. Repeatedly. But this time was different. I was so angry. Replaying all the instances of the fractured forgiveness cycle we had been operating in gave me a newfound sense of myself. I felt clearer than I had in a long time. I wanted him to feel the heat from me. And he did. The way this bitch ass nigga was skulking around like a mangy dog with his tails between his legs told me that he knew not to come for me. He was making no eye contact with me; he was peeking around the corners and he was not going to bed until he knew I was locked in the bedroom. I loved it. I lived for it. It's the least that could happen to him in light of all that had happened to me. Coupled with the fact that I hadn't said one single word to him. Not one. He didn't know what to expect and to be honest, I didn't truly know what to do. I assumed he had, by this time, heard from Erica. He made sure that I had what I needed in the house but outside of that he left me alone; a complete departure from the man who wouldn't think twice about choking me up or slapping me in the face on a whim especially if I chose to shut down on *him*. I didn't know if I should be terrified about how he was behaving or simply take it for what it was. I honestly didn't care because I didn't know what to think or what I was going to do. About any of it. There were so many things to dissect, so much to feel, so much to process. Why had I attracted this type of energy into my life? Twice! First in my relationship with Ty and now in my relationship with Troy. What was wrong with me? I've made some stupid decisions in life but what would warrant this? I had so many thoughts and questions running through my mind. *Breathe.*

Let's be clear here… my initial thought after the meeting with Erica was to call the police, period. I mean she had straight up admitted that she had stalked me, practically since high school. But I took a pause on that primarily because I needed to really piece things together. I mean, how had all of this come to be? And why was she so fixated on me? For all intent and purposes, she'd won. She broke me down, embarrassed the hell out of me, ran me out of town, and got her man. Why the fuck would she hold on to anything pertaining to me, after all this time? And what sick-ass individual takes such drastic measures to pursue someone in this way? For years! And then there was Troy. What in the entire fuck??? This nigga. I had no words. I mean, thinking back on it, he had been watching me at the resort in Cuba and she was obviously with him. But we've spent the last 6 years together. Through high highs and super lows, we've been together. He has seen the best and worst parts of me and vice versa. He has supported me, I supported him. He mistreated me, but I overlooked it. He hurt me, but I forgave him. But within the last year, something shifted for the better, or so I thought. I mean, after the situation with my parents, I'd been extremely raw and vulnerable and he'd been right there by my side. Taking care of me, encouraging me, and …… Stop it Lena!!! Fuck that shit!!!! This motherfucker is just as sick as this crazy bitch Erica!!! I snapped myself out of my fairy tale daze of how I wanted things to be and began to focus on how they actually were. I thought back on the previous relationship choices I'd made especially when I was with Ty. I took the intentional position of being the one in that relationship who took on all of the weight, carrying it all on my shoulders. He was in the limelight taking all the praise for his athleticism, good looks, and charisma while I was back cowering in the corner. I wasn't completely naïve I knew there were girls and groupies trying to get at him, but I convinced myself that despite all that was being thrown at him by these chicks, he only wanted me. So, I stayed regardless of what I heard through the grapevine, what I saw with my own eyes, and what had been told to me directly. I just took it all in and whisked it away, because no matter what I loved him and wanted to be with him even against my better judgment.

I'd done this throughout my entire relationship path… well, except during that ten-boy summer. Me, Ava and one of our other friends, Shavonne, spent an entire summer living our best, young adult lives. We'd either met or had already known these guys and let them wine, dine, and *whatever else* us until it was time to move on to the next one. It was so liberating to just *be* and have fun and that's exactly what we did. We didn't sleep with each guy we encountered or hung out with. But we did sleep with several of them. Sometimes more than once. We'd get together later and share notes about our escapades, including the highs and lows, and laugh until we were in tears. It was the best time ever. That's when Ava and I truly knew that we would forever be in each other's lives no matter what. You don't do some of the things that we had done and then not stay connected. We vowed to the other that some, no most, of the shit we did, would go to the grave. She was the only person, who knew that I was *buck wild* back then, good Lord. I let myself be open to some shit that I could never repeat to anyone else but

Ava. There were one-night stands, sometimes double/triple dips (*meaning I'd slept with multiple guys in the same day*), and truth be told we only used the moniker ten-boy summer because it sounded catchy. In actuality, we exceeded ten; easily. Now Shavonne was kicking with us as well and she knew some things, but Ava knew *all the things*. I would share the real deal with Ava because she was my girl, my sister, my ride-or-die. Hands down. But I digress.

Reflecting on it all as I tried to understand why I allowed and ultimately chose men like them into my life, I think what I came to realize is it was learned behavior. I know for certain that this is how Momma operated throughout her marriage to Dada. She would take it all and create an image for herself of what she wanted things to be amidst all of the chaos. All the lies, all the bullshit, all the cheating, all the abuse, all of it. She made excuses, and allowances, and paid for it all at her expense. Not this time. Not again. I was awake now, I wanted more. I deserved better. And goddamn it I was tired. To put it plainly, I was fucking pissed. And I was fucking pregnant. I needed help and I knew what to do. I needed to fucking call Ava.

It was 11:30 pm and I sat in my bedroom with the door locked and grabbed my cell phone. I dialed Ava's number and waited, praying she would pick up. It had been several years since we'd last spoken and I knew I was taking a gamble reaching out to her after all this time. The phone had rung almost 4 times, and I was about to hang up when I heard a soft sleepy "Hello" on the other end. I felt a warmth come over me and a big smile along with big crocodile tears. *Breathe*. "Bitch," I said into the phone. "Bitch," was her reply. And we were off. I told her everything. As I was telling Ava about it all I found myself immensely embarrassed.

"Lena, you need to get the fuck out of there. Where is he now? And where is this Erica bitch? Are they together? Do we need to fuck a bitch up? I'll kill that motherfucker." This was my Ava, always ready for anything at any time. We'd talked about it all and spoken so much about my shit that I hadn't even been able to ask her about the things that were happening in her life. But she shut that down, "Girl fuck all that, we got shit to take care of. You know I can't stand that nigga so I'm ready to come over now." And I knew she meant that, but I hadn't told her *everything*, everything. "Um, yeah I know boo, but um, there's something else. I'm pregnant." Ava didn't respond. In fact, there was a very long, awkward silence. "Hello?" I said. She said, "Lena, I love you. Always. But I can't do this with you if you aren't in the right headspace. Having a baby is a beautiful thing and I love that for *you*. But this man has abused you, lied to you, mistreated you, manipulated you, alienated you…" she stopped. I could hear her voice shaking and then she began crying softly into the phone. "For so long I sat back and watched you turn into someone that I no longer recognized, and as your best friend it became too much for me to watch and I couldn't take it any longer. So, as much as it hurt me, I walked away. You calling me now after all this time feels different and I truly, truly hope I'm right. I feel like I hear a conviction in your voice that reminds me of my Lena. I pray that in making this phone call it's your way of saying "*Sis I truly need you. Sis I'm back.* Is that what you're saying Lena? Because if it's not, then I wish you nothing but my sincere love and God's blessings. And I will hang up this phone, say a prayer for you as I always do and go back to sleep." I paused for a few seconds before responding with tears rolling down my cheeks. *Breathe in, breathe out, breathe in, breathe out.* I cleared my throat and said, "Sis, I truly need you. Sis, I'm back." I paused. *Breathe.* And then said, "And bitch, I said I was pregnant, not stupid." We laughed. We cried even more. And then we planned.

Ava and I talked for hours, well into the wee hours of the morning and I felt so much lighter by the end of our conversation. I was thrilled that she and I had reconnected even if for this disgusting reason. I mean, with me and Ava this was reminiscent of the way we'd always shown up for one another. There was much more to our friendship than just the bullshit related to these asshole men in our lives but this is when we would shine; in plotting and planning on how to get these niggas together. We fueled each other's fire and *checked* each other when necessary. I fucking loved this woman. Truly. Before we hung up, we'd planned to get together later in the week. She told me to get some rest and to make an appointment with the gynecologist. Ava and I argued a bit about the notion of me wanting to terminate the pregnancy. I wasn't certain what I was going to do yet. But I wanted to understand where things were in the pregnancy and what options were available to me. She respected that and just said, "Be open Lena, this is bigger than you and Troy." I received that, but I was still uncertain.

After our call, I'd rested the best I'd had since all this mess took place. I woke up hours later, well into the mid-morning and slowly started pulling the sheets back. I could smell coffee and something else cooking. "Ugh, why is he here," I said under my breath. I sat up and all of a sudden felt nauseous. I took a deep breath to try and settle myself. It didn't help and I ended up running to the toilet. I don't know if I can do this, I thought. I couldn't stand the idea of feeling this way each morning and to be brutally honest, I couldn't stand the idea of being pregnant by Troy. I'd heard Ava's comment about it being bigger than me and him but I was just being real. To me, it was about me and him. And at that moment, I wanted nothing more to do with him. I gathered myself, brushed my teeth and started the shower. I walked into the bedroom to grab some underwear, a t-shirt, and some sweatpants. I was rifling through my drawers and didn't come across anything that looked comfortable, so I opened Troy's chest of drawers to find something. I reached into the bottom drawer to pull out a pair of his sweatpants and felt papers, in a thick envelope. I grabbed the pants and the envelope and sat on the bed. The steam from the shower was billowing into the bedroom at this point; I'd forgotten I'd turned the shower on. I looked at the front of the envelope to see who the sender was. It said IL Department of Healthcare and Family Services; I felt sick again. I knew what this was, but I opened it anyway. The first page read, “INCOME WITHHOLDING FOR SUPPORT.” Then some sections read: Employer *Information of the Withholder, Employee Information of the Obligor, Order Information, Remittance Information* and there were pages and pages of legal jargon related to the enforcement of the child support order. I scanned the documents to see the date when this was originally filed. I thought, *Maybe he didn’t know. Maybe she was lying, and the timelines won’t add up. Maybe he didn’t truly participate in this with her, and she just used him to get to me.* I don’t know why I wanted to give him the benefit of the doubt. I knew better and the date really didn’t matter. In my heart, I knew better. But to satisfy my curiosity and skewed desire to find something/anything different I looked. The date indicated she’d filed the claim five years ago. Mica is 5 years old. That’s it. That’s all. Fucking bastard. I was extremely nauseated at this point. I threw the papers onto the bed and went into the bathroom, crying quietly. I stood at the sink for a moment and swiped the steam away from the mirror to see my broken, fractured self. It was all coming apart. *It's all good Lena. You got this. You will get this motherfucker. You will settle this*. I tried convincing myself of this as I gagged slightly and took a deep breath to calm myself. *Breathe in, breathe out, breathe*… Then I heard a knock on the bedroom door. I poked my head out and heard a knock again and heard Troy. "Lena baby. Lena. Please come to the door. Can we please talk?" I walked to the door and stood there for a few minutes. I was so disgusted by him. I felt sickened. I was so angry. I wanted to open the door and stab him right in the throat. I closed my eyes, took a deep breath, and opened the door. We stood there looking at each other for what seemed like an hour, it had been the first time I'd looked at him in over a week. He looked a mess. He hadn't shaved, he had on a t-shirt with food or coffee stains on it and his usually curly hair was all matted and lopsided. He stared hard at me in a way that would have normally made me fall into his arms. But I wasn't moved by it, and he could tell. There was a hardness and white-hot heat coming from every inch of me. He realized that time was of the essence so he cleared his throat and started to say something to me. His mouth was moving, and I assumed words were coming out but I couldn't hear anything. I held up my hand and I leaned forward and threw up on him. He stood there covered in the physical manifestation of how I felt about him, and I closed the bedroom door, locked it, walked into the bathroom, and took a long, relaxing shower. That was just the beginning of a long overdue but definite ending. My actions were fueled by a blinding rage in me that I had suppressed but it took this level of disgust, disrespect, and disregard to reawaken the beast. And she was back, without question. Lena Joi Timmons was back.

Thirteen: **Forward**

~onward so as to make progress; toward a successful conclusion~

-13-

I had not shared anything about the pregnancy with Troy, though I believed he suspected something. I had been unusually sleepy and could not hold anything down most mornings. It had been almost three weeks since the phone call from the doctor's office and I knew I had a small window of time to make a final decision on the pregnancy. I'd spoken with Ava about this several times and she was really routing for me to keep the baby. I was just extremely unsure about it given all that had happened. Troy was already planning to move out and understood there was no going back despite his incessant attempts to explain and apologize to me. The morning after I found the child support papers, I confronted him and told him this was just another nail in the coffin of this dead-ass relationship. He cried, groveled, and even tried to make himself throw up (I guess he thought that was a "thing" since I'd puked on him first); the man was ridiculously desperate. This nigga even had the nerve to suggest bringing Erica to the house so we could all "talk." I laughed so hard I peed on myself. Like seriously, what was he thinking? I stood there at that moment and saw him. I saw him for the pitiful man he was. He had allowed this other woman to manipulate him from the time they'd met and fell into her sick vendetta against me. For what? What did he gain from all this? Who knew what she had to pour into his pea-sized brain and ego to get him to go along with this diabolical rouse they played on me but not once did he stop it. Even after claiming that he loved me. Even after spending days and nights and long weekends and holidays and vacations with me. Not one time did he attempt to stop it. He had ample opportunity to completely cut her off and he did nothing. But while I can't try to rethink and replay all the aspects and moments of potential clarity for him, the clarity and opportunities were equally obvious to me as well. The moment he put his hands on me, I should have walked away. Period. But I did not. And it didn't happen once, it happened many times; even more times than I cared to recall. I had shared some of it with Ava and the times I didn't share with her, I knew she knew. She always knew. Hell, so did Momma and Dada. And Lenny. Oh, poor Lenny. He'd hated Troy from the moment he first met him and he never masked that feeling. I should've taken heed of that. Men know, you know? Lenny could sense the bullshit oozing from Troy's very being and he tried to let me know. But he tolerated Troy for me. And for some warped reason, I couldn't let him go. I wouldn't allow anyone to dictate what was right for me, and I also didn't want to have the responsibility of managing everyone else's expectations or feelings about my life choices. I mean I understand that people care and want the best for me, but my choices have an impact on one person ultimately, that's me. And now, potentially, this unborn child.

I was having a really hard day today. The nausea was unmatched and relentless. I tried to stay in bed and sleep it away, but I kept having to run to the bathroom to vomit. This is horrendous, I thought to myself. Who would want to do this all the time and is this what the rest of the pregnancy would be like? I didn't know if I was built for this. I finally mustered up the strength to shower and get dressed. I was starving but terrified to eat anything because all I could imagine was camping out next to the toilet afterward. Troy was in the kitchen cooking something that smelled amazing and despite my disdain for him, my belly and this baby led the way out of the bedroom and into the kitchen. One good thing about that man is he can cook. The smell of thick-cut bacon and cinnamon rolls wafted through the air into my nostrils and oddly made me a bit horny. *What the fuck*, I thought to myself. I just wanted a home-cooked meal, nothing more, nothing less. But when I got into the kitchen there he was standing there looking all pitiful. I gave a fake, half smile and asked, "Is there enough for me?" He smiled back with a big ol' Kool-aid grin, "Yeah, there's plenty. I'll make you a plate." He quickly grabbed a plate and piled on bacon, eggs, cinnamon rolls, and some sliced strawberries with powdered sugar sprinkled on top. He poured a cup of coffee with a glass of orange juice on the side and brought it all to me. I sat down a bit hesitantly but quickly began to devour the food on the plate in front of me. The lingering worry about nausea and vomiting went completely out the window. He sat across from me smiling like a Cheshire cat and it made me feel strange. I kept eating but then stopped mid-bite to ask, "What Troy?? Why are you staring at me like that??!" He took a sip of coffee and leaned back into his chair. "This is nice. It's been a long time since I've seen you. I mean really seen you, babe. You are so beautiful, Lena. Inside and out. If I could turn back time…" He paused and I could hear him choking up. But he stopped himself from shedding a tear. I think he knew that I wasn't going to be moved by it. Strangely, however, I was moved. I assumed it was the pregnancy hormones, but I was getting teary eyed too. I tried to keep my head down so he couldn't see but I couldn't stop the waterworks. I said, "Thank you, Troy. Thank you for the breakfast and for the compliment." We sat there together in silence as I finished breakfast, including the coffee and juice. He picked up the dishes and started to clean up. I excused myself, thanking him again, and went straight to the toilet to greet it.

When I came out of the bathroom, Troy was standing in the bedroom. "Lena, are you ok? Was it the food?" I sat down on the bed, partly from the exhaustion of heaving and partly from feeling overly emotional. I looked down at my feet and then said, "The food was delicious, Troy. At least it was for me. I don't think the baby likes it though." There was a long, uncomfortable silence that followed. I was afraid to look up from the floor but all I could hear was his breathing. It was fast and heavy. "The baby? The baby. Oh shit. You said baby? Is this why you've been so tired? Is this why.... Oh, shit you said baby. Oh shit." He walked away and I heard something coming from the living room that sounded like laughter. I was pissed. "I know this nigga isn't laughing at me right now", I said out loud. I mustered up the strength to stand and march into the living room and saw him sobbing uncontrollably. It was both disturbing and compelling and I was once again feeling horny. I stood there for a few minutes and then walked to him placing my hand on his head. He was holding his head in his hands and when I placed my hand on his head he grabbed it tightly. I was inclined to pull away but I didn't. Instead, I walked closer to him and he put his head against my stomach. I began to cry with Troy. God, what is happening right now? I thought to myself. I wanted to, no, I actually did hate this man. But more than that, I hated that I loved him so much and it's this love that compelled me to show him kindness in this moment. He pulled me toward him and I tried to refuse his gesture but I wanted it. I missed him. I wanted him. Troy stood up and grabbed me. We kissed and embraced so hard that it actually hurt, but I wanted him so badly. He rubbed all over my body and then roughly grabbed at my shirt pulling it over my head. He began to suck my breasts which were extremely tender and I moaned loudly at the pleasure it brought me. Instantly my cookie was wet, wetter than anytime before. He kept suckling my breasts and he, too, was moaning loudly. Then he said, "Lena baby, I'm so sorry.

I'm so sorry." He picked me up and took me to the bedroom and laid me on the bed gently. He slowly began to take off his clothes, looking at me the entire time. Troy's body was a masterpiece. Smooth chocolate skin, draped over mounds of muscle. I wanted to eat him alive. When he had completely disrobed, he began to pull my shorts down, then took off my panties. I was so wet; that I was almost unsure if I hadn't peed on myself. He put his face down there and nuzzled my cookie slowly. Taking small, calculated licks inside of me. I was writhing on the bed in sexual agony. Troy kept his eyes on me which made me both uncomfortable and hornier. With every lick, he'd look up at me to gauge my reaction and then go in even deeper and harder with his tongue. The bed was soaked and I was completely captivated by what was happening to me. Despite the hurt and pain I'd felt, I wanted this.

Once Troy had fulfilled his need and mine "down there in the cookie jar" he slowly made his way on top of me. He'd kissed every inch of me by this point and somewhere along the way, I'd become completely naked. I don't even recall when my clothes totally came off. We were both wet from sweat and God knows what else and then he was deep inside me. Lord have mercy I could have screamed. He felt so damned good. He was hard as a rock and his mouth was warm and moist on mine. His breathing was slow and labored and he spoke to me the entire time. "Lena, I love you. Lena, you feel so damn good. God, I've missed you. I will make it up to you." It all sounded irrelevant to me at that moment. I just wanted him. I wanted this. Just stay inside me this way, I thought. Stop talking. Keep fucking me. Please. Just keep fucking me and stop talking. For the next hour or so, that's what he did. He fucked me like his life depended on it. Every inch of him was mine and deeply planted inside of me. I wasn't thinking about him or the baby, I was just thinking about what this felt like for me. And it felt amazing. I stayed in it, laid in it for all it was worth. Without regret, without logic, without shame.

We both fell asleep at some point, and I woke up hours later. Troy was gone. I got up from the bed and went into the bathroom to clean up. I felt a strong bout of nausea return and took a couple of deep breaths and it soon passed. I took a long, hot shower, threw on some sweats and t-shirt, and went into the kitchen. The house was dark, Troy was nowhere to be found. I turned on the light in the kitchen and saw a note on the refrigerator. I grabbed it, and it said, "Lena, I have to say that today was both beautiful and confusing. I am going to stay away tonight. I want to talk tomorrow. I love you. Troy." I folded the note and sat it on the table. I grabbed some juice and an apple. He's right. Beautiful and confusing. That's us right now. I closed the refrigerator, went back into the bedroom, and watched TV until it watched me.

The next morning, I woke up to the smell of breakfast again. After my usual morning routine of vomit and mouthwash, I walked into the kitchen to see a plate filled with eggs, thick-cut bacon, and cinnamon rolls with strawberries and powdered sugar sprinkled on top. I sat down. Troy handed me a cup of coffee and poured the orange juice. We ate. We talked. We smiled and even laughed a few times. We cleared breakfast and the day went on. At a point later in the evening, we found ourselves back at the table together. We ate. We talked. We smiled and laughed even more. And then, we agreed to move forward. Together.

Fourteen: **Fear**

~an unpleasant emotion caused by the belief that someone or something is dangerous, likely to cause pain, or a threat~

-14-

I was finally at a place where I felt good, normal even. I was back to work, and the business was thriving. Dr. Moore and Nadia were thrilled to have me back and I didn't realize how much I'd missed them, my work, and seeing patients. I wasn't sure I'd be able to return after all the drama that had taken place late last year, but I felt good, and it felt right to go back. Perhaps it was the season, I always liked the transition from Winter to Spring. The sun is out longer, and the days just seem longer, and brighter. I loved leaving the office and sitting outside on the bench soaking up the sunshine. It wasn't very warm yet, temperature-wise, but the sun always made me feel good. I was beyond embarrassed about all that had taken place and equally embarrassed to return with an obvious *belly bump*. Dr. Moore and Nadia didn't bat an eye. They were screeching with excitement when I first walked back into the office. Once they realized I was expecting, the elation they displayed catapulted to a "whole '*nother level*' as my brother

Lenny would say. They didn't ask any questions about any of it, and even when I tried to apologize and explain the current state of the relationship they both stopped me. "Are you happy Lena?" I smiled, with tears forming in my eyes, "Yes, I am." "Then that's all that matters. You must be happy mentally so that you can bake a happy and healthy baby." Nadia said emphatically. We all smiled through our tears. I truly was happy. The happiest I'd been in forever. But not everyone felt the same.

Ava was NOT happy with my decision to stay with Troy. She was happy about the baby but she did not mince words when it came to her disdain for him and our "relationship". She did, however, commit to being there for me and the baby. No matter what. She told me and Troy that she had major concerns about us but respected our decision to put in the work and remain together. She was very blunt in her statements and inquiries. "*So where is old girl? Is she going to be popping up trying to disrupt y'all's relationship? Have you clearly communicated what the status of your and*

Lena's relationship is? What about the little girl? How will that be managed, because it's not her fault that her parents were behaving so recklessly. Will you still get to see her? How will the custody dynamic be structured? I hope you are truly in this for all the right reasons Troy because it's no secret that you are not a fan favorite of mine and I would hate to have to fuck you up." Troy took it all in stride. He'd already had to answer these same questions from Momma, Dada, and Lenny. He knew that nothing Ava said was out of line or coming from a place that was not centered on truth and genuine concern for me and the baby. He assured her that he loved me and was committed to showing me, her, my parents, and anyone else who questioned whether or not he was in this for the long haul. I sat there listening to Ava's rant and would periodically look up at Troy. I felt sorry for him. Ava was throwing verbal punches at him from the left and right. But I was also proud of him and equally proud of myself. We were taking the bull by the horns and being honest with each other in a way that I don't think we'd ever done. We were excited about this next chapter. This time was different. This time was going to be better than ever. This is what I kept telling myself but deep down inside I knew the truth.

Weeks later Troy met me at my doctor's appointment, and he was late. I was irritated and it showed in my face and body language. When he came rushing into the exam room I was already on the table. Today was the day we would find out the gender of the baby. We had discussed this appointment the night prior and Troy promised me he'd be there on time. He mentioned having a few meetings but assured me that he could move some things around and he would make it to the office on time. When he came in the doctor greeted him and he immediately went into this whole apology rant. I wasn't trying to hear it. I was annoyed and embarrassed. The doctor chuckled saying, "No worries, Mr. Bowers, it happens all the time." She said if she had a nickel for every time a new dad came rushing in late, she'd be a billionaire. Troy laughed. I did not. He walked over to me, said "Hey babe, I'm so sorry but I'm here now" and leaned down to try and kiss me. I turned away. He grabbed my hand and squeezed it, hard. Really hard. Tears instantly welled up in my eyes, but I tried to play it off blaming it on the images the doctor was showing us from the ultrasound. She'd taken several of them but couldn't get a clear shot of the baby to be able to tell us if it was a girl or boy. Troy was becoming visibly frustrated by this and the doctor picked up on the shift in his energy. She said, "Let me try one last thing, hang on." She applied more of the gel to my belly then pushed and massaged it and took one last image. "There it is you guys. Do you see that? It's a BOY!" she exclaimed. Troy let go of my hand and squealed like a little girl. I immediately burst out laughing. He shot me a harsh look and I tried to recover by shifting the initial reaction and said, "Oh my goodness, I'm so happy. Troy, it's a BOY! A beautiful boy!" I smiled with tears in my eyes. He smiled back at me. But something was off.

In the car on the way home, I was purposely trying to avoid speaking to Troy. His energy was off and it was obvious but I didn't want that to overshadow this amazing moment between us. We rode along for a while before he finally said, "I apologize for being late. I didn't intend to be." I said softly, "It's ok baby, I knew you'd get there eventually." We rode along a little further and he turned the music up loudly on the radio. I was looking at the ultrasound images, still amazed at how many had been taken before we got to the last one to finally find out the baby's gender. The doctor took at least 14 images. Troy pulled off the road turned into a gas station and asked if I wanted anything. I asked for a bottle of water. He went inside the store, and I called Ava. She immediately said,

"Bitch what is it, a niece or nephew?" I burst out laughing. I said, "Start buying Tonka trucks auntie A!" She screamed in excitement. "I knew it!!!! You don't need no damn girl. Ooh, Lena, I can't wait to spoil him! What did the jackass say? I'm sure he's thrilled." I told her that he seemed happy, but his energy and behavior were off. I told her that he had come late to the appointment. "See, that's that bullshit. Stupid ass. Ugh, I can't stand that motherfucker. I'm sorry Lena, I'm trying, I swear I am, but he gotta do better. There is no room for error in this. Not now, not ever as far as I'm concerned, or his ass will be OUT." She went on to say that we were entering into new and unchartered territory as parents and that our revamped relationship needed to be solid. She was right about it all and I wasn't about to argue. Not one lie was told and I just wanted to bask in the glow of my reality. *I am about to be someone's mother*; I thought to myself. I closed my eyes for a second to breathe and take that in. This is why I loved Ava. She held me down but would also keep it real with me. Straight, no chaser. Her delivery could be harsh and bristling at times, but I knew it came from her unapologetic and unwavering love for me. I leaned back into the seat and we kept chatting about all things baby when Troy walked up to the car and flung my door open. Startled by his behavior I sat up and said, "Hey, let me call you back when I get home," I hung up before waiting for Ava to respond. "What's wrong with you? Why did you open the door like that?" Troy shoved the bottle of water into my chest hard and then slammed the passenger door. Tears welled up in my eyes again as I held my hand up to my chest which was throbbing. *Breathe in. Breathe out. Breathe in. Breathe out.* Troy pumped the gas, slammed the gas cap closed, and then got into the car. I tried to hide the tears by turning my head away from him. He reached over and I flinched. He snatched the ultrasound photos and placed them in his lap. Then he started the car, turned the music up super loud and we proceeded to drive home, not saying a word to each other. My heart was racing a mile a minute, and I stared out the window trying to center myself and focus on my breathing. I had no clue what had triggered this behavior in him, but history had taught me to remain quiet and to keep still. *God, please make this go away*, I prayed to myself in silence. When we pulled into the driveway, he got out quickly and then walked over to my door, opening it fast.

"Come on inside," he said holding out his hand to help me. I took his hand, and we went inside the house. I had no idea what was happening with him, and I was terrified to ask so I walked to the bedroom to get something comfortable to change into. I decided to take a quick shower first and went into the bathroom to start the water. *I need to wash this weird energy from me and calm myself down*, I whispered under my breath. I wasn't sure where Troy was or what he was doing but I figured I'd give him some time to settle himself. Hopefully, he would take in the excitement of the baby news and relax. I assumed he wanted to reach out to his family and share the news since he had taken the ultrasound pictures from me. We had initially decided that we would keep the baby's gender to ourselves, even though I'd already shared it with Ava. But then we said, "Fuck it, let's tell everyone." Immediately I thought he may have been angry that I shared the news first, but Troy knew that I would tell Ava so it couldn't be that. I just wasn't sure what he was so agitated about. I stepped in the shower and the water felt amazing on my face. Soon I found myself standing underneath the shower head letting the warmth of the water run over me. I was standing in the same spot for a long time simply rubbing my belly and smiling. This felt so surreal. *I am about to be a mother*. I thought about how much my mother poured into me and my brother and I wanted to be the same kind of mom to my child. Even when things felt uncertain between her and Dada, she always made us feel safe and secure. I wanted that for our child. I prayed that Troy and I would find our rhythm again, be a strong couple, and better parents. I felt so overwhelmed by all of this and then the tears began to flow. Thinking about this new reality was hitting me hard and before I knew it, I was sobbing. This wasn't sadness though; it was just pure joy and raw emotion. A much-needed emotional release.

After some time, I finally stepped out of the shower and was startled to see Troy sitting on the chair of the vanity. He had a large bath towel in his hand and told me to come to him. I walked over slowly, and he wrapped me up in the towel. This felt awkward and a bit uncomfortable, and I wanted to ask him what was going on. Given how erratic his behavior had been since we left the doctor's appointment I was confused. He was like Dr. Jekyll and Mr. Hyde. What had I done to cause this erratic behavior shift toward me? The Psychiatrist in me wanted to understand. But I was physically tired and figured I would just go with his current flow. He began to dry me off, and at first, I giggled because he was focused on my belly area. It felt as though he was fooling around but then he became increasingly forceful and aggressive. He pulled me back and forth vigorously and continued to rub in the towel in the same area on my back until it burned. "Troy stop, you're hurting me!" I screamed. I tried to pull away, but he grabbed me by my hair and threw me onto the floor holding me down. He didn't say one word. I was shocked, scared, and struggling to breathe. *Relax Lena*, I said to myself. *Breathe in. Breathe out. Breathe in. Breathe out.* He pulled quickly at his pants and without hesitation, he entered me so hard that I screamed. He thrust himself inside me repeatedly until I felt like I was going to pass out. I kept wriggling, trying to free myself but to no avail. He was too strong. He stood up and grabbed my hair again, dragging me into the bedroom. The carpet was burning my legs from the force of my trying to fight against him and then he violently turned me around entering me from behind. I finally mustered up the breath in my lungs to ask him to stop. Even through the immense pain, I tried to speak calmly, but he ignored my pleas. He slammed my face into the floor, and I instantly felt warmth from the blood seeping from my now busted lips. I cried out, “Troy, please stop. You’re hurting me. You’re hurting the baby.” He did not stop. He still did not say one word. Instead, he pushed my face harder into the carpet and continued to rape me. Repeatedly. I screamed and tried fighting back but he used so much force to subdue me that I eventually stopped resisting. I simply stopped. *Breathe in. Breathe out. Breathe in. Breathe out.* I must have blacked out because when I came to, I was propped against the wall. I tried to stand, but my legs were limp. I was in pain all over my body, and I soon realized that I was bleeding from my vaginal and rectal areas. There was a stabbing, sharp pain in my stomach, and I suddenly felt nauseous. I threw up violently all over myself and the floor. I tried to gather myself and looked around to see where Troy was, but I could only turn my head slightly before feeling dizzy and nauseous again. He wasn't in the room, initially, so I began working to stand myself up. I placed my hands against the wall, took a deep breath, and pushed with all my might to stand. I kept losing my balance and gagged repeatedly. Blood and saliva were oozing from my mouth and I peed on myself. Then I heard footsteps coming towards me and as I tried even harder to pull myself up, I collapsed and blacked out again. When I came to this time, I was on the floor and felt the most horrific pain in my pelvic area. I kept blinking to clear my blurred vision only to realize Troy was violently jamming something inside of me. It was the most excruciating pain I'd ever felt, and I screamed and kicked my legs as best as I could. I was trying to say, "Please stop, please stop," but the words came out like gibberish. He was intentionally trying to make me lose this baby. The tears were blinding me, and I could not catch my breath. Then he punched me in the stomach so hard that I blacked out again. The next thing I remember Troy was grabbing me by the neck and slamming me headfirst into the dresser. My head crashed against the mirror, breaking it, and slicing my forehead open. As the blood poured over my face, I realized that I could no longer speak. I was moving my mouth, but nothing was coming out and I was going in and out of consciousness. There are also moments I recall being kicked in the stomach and back repeatedly. Waves of pain and sobbing and darkness overcame me. He sodomized me at least four times and stood over me laughing. In my mind, this went on forever. As I lay there, I replayed the weeks, days, hours, minutes, and seconds of the time we'd spent together, to try to understand why this was happening and what brought this on. The conclusion is this was simply who Troy always was, who he has always been. This is the sick person that lived beneath the façade he presented to everyone who encountered him. He had shown me on more than one occasion that he could be violent and irrational. He had shown me who he was, but I thought we had grown past it, and I believed him when he said never again, Lena. I believed him when he said he would *do the work* to *make this work*. He told me that we were moving forward together. Lies, all disgusting lies.

When he wasn't forcefully jamming himself or the "foreign object" inside me, he was beating the hell out of me with whatever he could get his hands on. I later learned that the foreign object was a metal, long-handle cooking spoon from our kitchen. I was being ripped apart by the man I loved and trusted. The man I poured my entire being into. I did not know this man. This wasn't a man; this was an animal. That is what the experience felt like, being torn apart by a ravenous dog who was uncontrollable and untamed. Every single effort I made to get him to stop failed. I screamed and begged and pleaded with him. I asked him to leave. I told him I loved him. Told him I would forgive this. Just begged him to please stop. He did not. He continued this vicious and animalistic attack until he felt satisfied and finally stopped. I lay there on the floor barely breathing. I lost time, could not move, and was repeatedly going in and out of consciousness. Before I passed out for the final time, I heard him talking on the phone as he stood over me. He said casually, "Hey, are ya'll dressed? Okay baby, I'm on my way. Tell Mica Daddy on the way. See you soon. Love you." And then he walked out and left me there on the bedroom floor bruised, beaten, and covered in blood and vomit.

Fifteen: **Frantic**

~ wild or distraught with fear, anxiety, or other emotion ~

-15-

Momma, Dada, Lenny, and Ava were in the family room at Northwestern Memorial Hospital waiting for the doctors to come to them with an update on my condition. I had been in surgery for the last 5 hours. By God's grace, I had mustered up enough strength to get to my cell phone and call 911 before passing out one final time. When my family was notified, they were told that I had been found lying on the floor of my bedroom in a massive pool of blood. The police told my parents not to come to the house because the room looked like a scene from a horror movie. They said it appeared I had been violently attacked, assuming sexual and physical assault. They did not share much over the phone but told my parents that I was unresponsive and being taken straight to the hospital. Momma asked if I was breathing, and she was told "Yes" but it was shallow. Now, what they would later come to learn was I had been violently raped and viciously assaulted with a foreign object. The doctors would later confirm that I had suffered a miscarriage as a result of the attack, and my internal organs were severely damaged requiring emergency surgery to stop the internal bleeding. I had sustained what the doctors called, "*The most horrific and significant vaginal, perineal, and rectal injuries*" anyone had ever seen in their entire medical career. I had a deep laceration across my forehead that would require reconstructive surgery. I suffered a major concussion, a knee fracture, a dislocated shoulder, and a broken wrist. I had also severely strained my vocal cords to the point of having difficulty speaking, breathing, and swallowing for several months post-surgery. I was in really bad shape.

Momma and Dada anxiously sat for hours in the hospital family room waiting for the doctors to tell them something about my situation. It was the first time they had spent any time together since the revelation about Dada's "other" son all those months ago. They were still living in the same house together, but Momma hadn't been able to move past this one. Dada had a tally list as long as a city block of women he'd cheated with but none of those conquests produced a living, breathing person. So this revelation had a completely different effect on her and she couldn't process it, at least not now. Despite their uneasiness with one another, they put that aside to be there for me. I was all they were focused on. Nothing else mattered. They sat next to each other, held hands, hugged one another, prayed together, and even cried together. Dada was so attentive to Momma, ensuring he would make her as comfortable as he could no matter how bad things seemed. They didn't know much but they could both tell by the way the ER doctor spoke that things looked pretty grim. They hung on to every word he said, "*She is breathing, but barely. She is badly injured and in a critical state. She will need emergency surgery. We cannot determine the outcome at this juncture, but we will do everything we can to save her. Please be seated. Please be patient. Please know that she is in the best place she can be at this time.*" No parent wants to ever experience or be part of a conversation like this one.

Momma and Dada sat down, held on tightly to each other and they waited.

Ava and Lenny, on the other hand, were not as calm or patient. They both paced back and forth in the family room, trying to keep it together. They both wanted to kill Troy. They proclaimed it out loud. “That nigga did this to her! I knew he wasn’t shit. I told her to leave his ass! I told her!” Ava ranted these statements repeatedly and went from inconsolable crying to visible bouts of anger. She could not contain herself on either side of the emotional spectrum she was on. She was either biting her cuticles, slamming her fist against the wall, or sitting on the floor in the corner sobbing. She knew Troy was no good. She’d tried to tell Lena this over and over again. “Why didn’t she listen to me,” she said talking to herself. “I told her he wasn’t shit; I knew he wasn’t shit. I will kill this motherfucker. I will KILL HIM!” Ava always felt something bad was going to happen, she almost waited for it. So, when she received the frantic call from Momma, she knew this was it. Momma was screaming into the phone, "*My baby, my baby, he almost killed my baby!! Get here, Ava, get here!*" Ava hung up the phone. She was angry. She wanted to kill Troy, right then. Ava went to her bedroom and paced back and forth. She called her boyfriend, Marcus, but got his voicemail. She slipped on her shoes, grabbed her purse, and headed for the door. Then she stopped. She turned around and went into the hallway closet to grab the gun safe from the top shelf. She placed her finger on the biometric pad and the safe beeped. She opened it and grabbed her gun. It was a small, compact Beretta Tomcat. She briefly recalled when we had gone to the range to shoot at targets. I was not really interested in going and had no intention on shooting, but Ava was like "Bitch please, we doing this. Gotta know how to air a nigga out." We had so much fun that day and we both ended up buying our guns. The exact same type and brand. We were so proud and felt so empowered. But in this moment, Ava felt anything but empowered. She felt anger, hatred, and despair. Ava cried as she placed the gun in her purse and walked to her car.

"I'm going to kill this motherfucker," she said out loud. Before she could pull away from her house and make what would have been a horrible decision, her phone rang. It was Lenny. Through her tears, she answered the phone, "Where are you?" Lenny's tone was clear and eerily calm. "I'm in my car, sitting in front of Lena's house. I'm 'bout to kill this nigga A." Ava snorted and said, "Bro, I just put my piece in my purse. Let's do this." Lenny said, "I've been sitting here since Dad called me. I know I should be at the hospital but if this motherfucker walked right out now, I would blow his motherfucker brains out." Ava said, "Yeah, I know. I had the same idea, but he won't be at the house. At least not right away, if ever. He knows what he's done. Shit for all he knows, she's dead." When Ava finished that statement, she began to process what she had just said and then screamed into the phone. Lenny told her to stay there. He started his car and headed to Ava's house. She was in no condition to drive or think or do anything. Ava was completely destroyed. The mere thought of potentially losing me was too much for her to handle. She sobbed the entire time, right there in the car until Lenny pulled up behind her. She finally got herself together, got out of her car, and headed to Lenny's. When she pulled on the door handle, she realized it was locked so she tapped on the window and peered in. Lenny was just sitting there, frozen. No expression on his face and staring straight ahead. Ava tapped again. Click. Finally, he unlocked the door.

Lenny drove like a bat out of hell to get to Ava. He was running lights and cutting corners like a NASCAR driver. In his mind, he couldn't fathom a world that didn't have me in it. We were each other's lifeline. Since we were little, we always protected and looked out for one another. "How could this be real?" he thought. Lenny had an unhealthy habit of suppressing his emotions so from the moment he'd spoken to Dada and learned what happened his mind was racing. He didn't cry even as Dada struggled to get the words out. "Get here, son. We're at Northwestern. She's in really bad shape. That sick ass nigga did this. He beat her to a bloody, lifeless pulp. I don't know if she will...." Lenny stopped him, "Dada, I'm coming," and hung up the phone. The way Lenny's emotional processing works is he takes in the situation, marinates on all aspects of what is occurring, and then has a delayed but visceral reaction. When he was a child, he was bullied a lot and as a result of that he would bottle up the emotion until it reached a dangerous boiling point. The reaction would then present itself as pure, unmanageable rage. So, the place he was in in this instance was just that, pure unadulterated rage. He wanted to hurt Troy badly. He wanted to remove him from this world. When Lenny was driving to Ava, he was fueled by this rage; he was almost in a daze and before he knew it, he was parked behind Ava's car. Getting to her was a blur but somehow he was there, parked in front of herr house. He sat behind the wheel staring straight ahead with all kinds of scenarios running through his mind. *What the fuck happened? I thought they went to see the OB /GYN today to learn the sex of the baby. Where is this motherfucker? He must know that he's going to die. He left my sister for dead. Dada said she was barely breathing. I'm gonna kill this nigga. I'm gonna kill this nigga. I swear to God I'm gonna ki....* He stopped mid-thought. "What the fuck is that tapping noise?" he'd heard himself say aloud. He looked over and realized it was Ava tapping on the car window. She had been trying to open the door, but it was locked. He pressed the unlock button and Ava got in. Ava and Lenny looked at each other for a long time and finally embraced. They held each other, both trembling with undeniable emotion and then sat in silence before Lenny finally started the car to head to the hospital. One single tear fell from his eye, and he quickly wiped it away. Visibly shocked by this reaction from Lenny, Ava began to cry quietly. As Lenny pulled off, he felt Ava's hand grab his. Lenny allowed the tears to flow. This was the first time he'd allow himself to cry, about anything. But to Lenny, I was worth it.

Sixteen: **Functional**

~ of or having a special activity, purpose, or task; relating to the way in which something works or operates ~

-16-

I remained in the hospital for almost five months undergoing several surgical procedures, occupational, mental health and physical therapies, and recovery. I had to then go to rehab for another three months to rebuild my mental and physical strength. The extent of my injuries was severe, and it was nothing but God's grace and mercy that allowed me to survive. He showed his favor and gave me the strength I needed to make that fateful call to 911. Troy's bitch ass had left me there for dead and likely believed he succeeded in killing me. But God said Not So! There were many times post-surgery when I wished I had died. The road to recovery was a long and painful one indeed. The physical damage was hard to believe and harder to explain. I had suffered a miscarriage, and my fallopian tubes and uterus had been damaged in several places. This resulted in the doctors making the heart-wrenching decision to perform a total hysterectomy on me. I had to have reconstructive surgery on my face to repair the deep laceration across my forehead, which had been cut open from left to right. My left eye socket had been shattered and my jaw was broken so surgical procedures were performed to address those injuries. I lost the top two front teeth and had to have dental implants installed. I had bitten through my top lip and lost a small piece of my tongue. My left wrist and right ankle were fractured, and my left shoulder was deeply bruised from the dislocation. I had 6 broken ribs, and my kidneys were severely bruised. I had to have three blood transfusions and was completely covered in dark blue and black bruises, from head to toe. There was also a huge chunk of my hair missing from the back of my head. I was a hot mess.

I was fortunate to have had an amazing team of nurses, physicians and therapists who tended to my every need and did their absolute best to fix what had been broken. Momma and Dada were there around the clock, from sunup to sundown every single day without fail. They encouraged me, cried with me, fed me, bathed me, combed my hair, prayed with me, and prayed for me. Every single day. Bless their hearts because I was not a good patient at all, and did not make it easy for them most days. I was angry, I was sad, I was confused, I was irritable and I was undoubtedly depressed. There was a Social Worker assigned to come and talk with me about my mental and physical support options, but I was defiant and downright nasty. "Ma'am/Sir please don't come in here trying to therapize or tell me what I need. You don't know me. I do this for a living and guarantee I've got more credentials than you. I'm good. Get the fuck out of here with that shit! Bye." Momma or Dada would usually follow the person I'd yelled at to apologize for my outbursts. Then I'd turn on them. "Y'all can go too. I don't need anyone to take pity on me. I'm ok. I'll heal, eventually. Life will go on. Or maybe it won't. Just leave, please!" But they wouldn't. They would listen to me vent, scream, and cry but they would sit right where they were. Every single day. They would not give up on me.

Initially, I refused to see Ava and Lenny for weeks. When they showed up in the hospital room, I would pretend to be asleep. Eventually, I told the head Nurse they were not allowed to come into my room at all. I remember hearing Ava yell from the hallway, "Fuck you mean she said I'm not allowed in? Lena! Lena! It's A!" Then I heard Momma say, "Ava just go home baby. I'll call you. I promise. Just give her time." I didn't want to see them, and I certainly didn't want them to see me. Not this way. I knew what it would do to them. Lenny's response was almost identical to Ava's. He ranted and raved until hospital security threatened to have him escorted out. I heard him say to someone, "Put your motherfucking hand on me again bitch, see what happens." Even in immense pain I couldn't help but chuckle. This is why I made the decision not to see them right away. Imagine what would happen if they walked in and saw the monster I had morphed into. Both Ava and Lenny had a temperament that could cause them to make irrational knee-jerk decisions. Momma and Dada had sustained enough pain and turmoil, and I could not allow anything else to cause them more worry. It was all too much. I knew this was deeply hurtful for Lenny and Ava, but I also knew deep down they understood where I was coming from. So, we didn't see or speak to each other until I was well into the second month of hospitalization.

I began physical therapy as soon as I was able and it was a grueling experience. I hated my physical therapist with a passion. Not literally, it was more so situational. Therapy hurt like hell and I was, on most days, still not mentally ready to accept what had gotten me here. My physical therapist was actually a Godsend. He was patient, he was kind, but he was extremely thorough. He held me accountable for doing the work to recover. He would push me beyond what I told him I was capable of doing. That's what I hated about him. His name was Joe. He would make me walk the halls and get in/out of the bed on my own. I'd cry and say, "Joe, please I can't do this. Joe, this really hurts. Joe, I hate your fucking guts." No matter what I'd say to him or how much I complained, his response was always the same. "OK. You got this Lena. Let's go." I fucking hated him. But he knew what I needed, and he wasn't going to deviate from the treatment plan. He also knew that I was in a deep state of depression while still trying to put on a brave face for everyone. I protested sitting for a mental health consult for at least 3 weeks before he finally got me straight. We were wrapping up a long therapy session one day and I lost my balance, falling into the mirrored wall of the room. I yelped a bit because my ribs were still sore and asked him for help to stand. He looked at me and said, "Oh, so you do need help from others, huh? Why not take *all* the help that is being offered to you Lena? Yes, of course, I will help you at this moment. As will the occupational therapist in a few weeks when you're released. As will the mental health therapist. I see people all the time block themselves from the blessings placed before them and I shake my head in disbelief. We all fall, Lena. Each one of us. And it's ok to ask for and take the help being offered. It doesn't make you "less than". It makes you human. You are in a vulnerable place right now but there is not one day that your family and friends aren't here to help you. You are blessed to have that. You are also blessed to have the resources available to you for this type of support. Let us do our best to help you. To work to the best of our ability to assist you in becoming functional again." He grabbed my hand, helped me stand up, and said, "OK. You got this Lena. Let's go." I stood up, choking back my tears, and walked to my room, leaning in on Joe a little more than usual.

Within the next several weeks, I was finally seeing a mental health professional. I honestly was still resistant in the beginning; intentionally guarding myself from being open, honest, and vulnerable. The shit is hard, to completely say out loud all the things about your life's experiences that are real and hard and complicated and sad and traumatic. I thought I was ready, but I wasn't. At least not in the first few sessions. Then one day that changed. My therapist and I needed to find our *rhythm* and she took an approach in this particular session that cracked me wide open. She simply asked me to talk about the first childhood memory that came to mind. Without even hesitating I began to speak about the night Dada and Momma were fighting in the hallway when I was 5 years old. I shared details with her that I had never uttered to anyone. The words and details of that experience were graphic, hard to say, and harder to accept. But it had been my reality. It all began with that childhood experience. I had convinced myself that I'd gotten over it. What I came to understand was that experience informed every future experience I would have. I had simply pushed that shit down. Buried it somewhere deep inside of myself. We are taught to believe that when something is buried, it's dead. Technically that is true but the ghosts of those experiences, the overall trauma, the smells, the sounds, the power; they all remain. I'd learned that I was like a zombie walking through my life. I'd minimized myself when it came to all that I had achieved yet I show up for others giving of myself, even at my own expense. Despite the notion of having a buttoned-up and pulled-together image (as my father had instilled in Lenny and me) beneath that façade, I was a sad and fractured little girl. I was still stuck in that 5-year-old little girl's reality. I had mastered the ability to put on the "strong, black woman" persona and "*do the things*," "*be that chick*," "*take no shit*," "*achieve anything I put my mind to*." I could do that any day of the week. And I was great at it, but it was all a big ol' pile of bullshit. In reality, I didn't know how to praise myself. I didn't know how to show up for myself. I didn't know how to say I needed help. I didn't know how to say no. I didn't know how to stop taking care of other people. It was easier for me to immerse myself in this behavior because it kept me from looking at myself in the mirror and seeing that broken little girl. I busied myself with school, work, men, and friends but I avoided taking care of myself. I chose all the wrong men for what I thought were the right reasons. I saw more in them than they saw in themselves and made it my mission to "*fix*" them. Yet despite my efforts, the only consistent things in my life were the patterns of lies, abuse, and infidelity. My therapist asked once, "Why do you think you've chosen these types of men? The ones who lie and cheat and abuse? Where has this behavior shown up in your life?" Instantly, I became defensive. "What are talking about? I have never experienced…" I stopped mid-sentence. I leaned back onto the sofa, covered my face with the pillow next to me, and began to cry. A deep guttural sobbing cry. I moved the pillow from my face and said, "Dada. For as much as I hated what he did to Momma, I inadvertently absorbed every aspect of his disgusting, disrespectful, and deplorable behavior towards women. Consequently, I became the living, breathing model of the woman I vowed never to be." I was cracked wide open. Fully exposed. We had lots of work to do. In the infamous words of my friend Joe, I said to myself, "OK. You got this Lena. Let's go."

Seventeen: **Free**

~ not under the control or in the power of another; able to act or be done as one wishes ~

-17-

One of the most appealing things, in my opinion, about living in the Midwest is the transition that occurs from season to season. My favorite is the change from Summer to Fall. The leaves start to change color, and the temperatures are generally more predictable and milder. You can drive through areas of the city like Hyde Park, take Cottage Grove, and then cut through Washington Park to experience the Fall transition in all its majesty. Leaves appear in the most beautiful shades and hues of brown, orange, and yellow litter the streets and it's simply magical. There's a crispness in the air that seemingly makes it feel like breathing is easier. It made me feel alive and happy, even free. It took me back to my childhood when Dada would rake the leaves and Lenny, and I would run and dive into the piles. Life was so easy then. Carefree. We didn't worry about anything, ever. At least nothing of real substance. Life was simpler, lighter. This is what the Fall season reminds me of, and I wish I could bask in the glow of this feeling always. The previous year had been riddled with so much heartache, intense healing, and thankfully a renewed focus on moving ahead with my life. Therapy strengthened my belief in life again. I felt that I was armed with the tools I needed, and the softness of the Fall season gave me a sense of empowerment to do just that.

I had been in therapy now for almost a year and was feeling better mentally than I had in many, many years. I was seeing my therapist weekly because I had a lot to unpack. Childhood shit, relationship shit, family shit, Dada shit, Momma shit, work shit, and, of course, ME shit. It all came back to me in the end. I can now accept and embrace that fact. For the predominance of my life, I pretended to be unbothered or strong, or unfazed by things, but it was all a charade. I had mastered the ability to show up in the way I needed to get things done, to persuade and influence, to essentially fool the people I encountered into believing I had it together. It was all fake. I didn't realize that I didn't know who I was. I was an imposter. It took me back to high school and the uneasy feelings I had about the friend group I was a part of. I didn't really know them, and they certainly didn't know me. But we would collectively band together to present a made-up image for those around us. None of which would have been as impactful if we had to stand alone. I can guarantee that. Standing alone meant having to identify with something. It meant having to show up as your true authentic self and I had no clue who that person was then any more than I do now. Therapy was uncovering and unraveling all of this for me. I realized life had been blurry for me. I didn't truthfully remember a lot of what transpired in my life; at least not the aspects that truly mattered. I could tell you about the encounters with the men in my life and the relationship bullshit. But I couldn't tell you much about taking classes, meeting people in school, working the various roles I've held, or accomplishing all that I had. I didn't have working memories of some of the most important occurrences of my life. That made me sad because I could show proof of the hard work I'd put in. The various degrees and certificates I'd attained hang on the wall in my office. I established meaningful personal and professional relationships with people who played a significant part in my journey. I sit on the Board of various organizations and have spoken to people and communities about the importance of Mental Health in the African American community. I've been a staunch proponent and advocate for Black babies and worked hard to create support models and identify resources to aid in meeting health and wellness needs for the impoverished. I've written countless journal articles and publications on this topic. I've written a book and received an honorary doctoral degree from Howard University in Mental Health Advocacy. I have, *humbly*, done some amazing things in my life. Yet it's all a blur. My mental health had never been at the forefront of my life journey and for that, I have suffered.

When I was finally released from the hospital, I decided as part of my healing journey to move out of the house I had shared with Troy. My therapist agreed that it would not be a healthy choice to stay in a place that presented so much trauma for me. Initially, I stayed with Momma and Dada because I was still seeing an occupational therapist and needed their support. It was nice being doted on by my parents and equally nice to experience them sharing in the responsibilities. They seemed different, more at ease with each other. I even noticed small signs of affection between them from time to time. Dada would rub Momma's shoulders when she was standing at the kitchen sink. Momma would lean in and give Dada a small peck on the cheek if he was sitting at his desk. They would sit close together to watch the news, with Momma's leg draped over Dada. I liked this version of them. But I hated the tragedy that essentially was the catalyst of their newfound connection; nonetheless, it was beautiful to witness.

I decided to downsize my new living space and opted for a smaller, ranch style home in the Western Suburbs of Chicago. My injuries had impacted me in ways that would make it difficult to do things like walk up and down stairs.

Dada was hoping I would choose something like a condo in the city, but I didn't want to be near the hustle and bustle of downtown, at least not right now. I wanted an area that would take me away from all the triggers and reminders of my life with Troy but also offer me the peace and comfort of a new and beautiful beginning. My new home has 3 bedrooms and 2.5 bathrooms with a large, fenced backyard. The street was tree-lined and quiet. There was shopping nearby and countless restaurants to choose from. The most amazing aspect of the move is that I could see patients in the area close to my home. Years ago, Dr. Moore opened a practice in this area, and we had discussed the possibility of me taking it on at some point. She enjoyed being in the city and, for a time, so had I. But I was ready for this change. I needed it. I had learned through therapy that I thrived in situations that challenged me professionally but, in the past, I had used those challenges to avoid dealing with personal ones. This time it would be different. There was still work to be done and countless sessions in therapy, but now I was present. Now I was more aware and utilizing the tools and recognizing the triggers.

Lenny and Dada, along with a few friends, managed move-in day like champs leaving me, Momma and Ava to sit back and enjoy cocktails on the patio. In all actuality, it was Dada who told us to "*go sit down somewhere*" because we were "*talking too much* and *getting in their way.*" We did not protest, in fact, we bee-lined to the fridge to grab the champagne I'd had chilling since early that morning. Ava squealed and clapped her hands when she saw me pouring the glasses. "Yes honey, pour it up!" Momma shook her head and giggled to herself. This was it; this was exactly what I'd hoped would become my reality. A fresh start, surrounded by my family. I felt amazing in this new space, it was definitely all coming together. All I could think about was decorating and tending to my yard; even painting again. I hadn't considered painting since I was in high school. The thought of it made me anxious all of a sudden. *How had I lost sight of doing what made me happy*? Then the question shifted to *why*. The simplest response that I could muster was this deep seeded passion of mine got lost in the shuffle of my complex life. My creativity became stunted amidst all of the other moving parts of my life. I put family first. I put school first. I put my relationships first. I put work first. Now I had time to revisit what I wanted for the first time in a very long time. I have time now to reset the entire thing. But I need to do it in a way that makes sense, that's realistic and practical. My therapist would constantly remind me to pace myself. "Lena, you tend to have an idea about something and then make a knee jerk decision about it without fully thinking it through. How has that worked out for you so far?" That stung a little, but she was right. That had been my pattern, all my life. I identify something and run with it in a frenzy, and I don't always take time to weigh out the pros and cons. Instead, I just go with it usually to accommodate others to prove to them that I am supportive, or that I care. Essentially, I'm people pleasing. This behavior is a symptom of anxiety. As a clinician, I knew this and assessed these very behaviors in my patients but for some reason, I could not recognize it in myself. Granted, not all decisions I've made have been bad ones. I had established a pretty good life for myself in many areas, romantic relationships aside. Now it was time to begin again, heal myself from the inside out, and live life fully with a primary focus on making myself happy. That's where I tended to struggle. Learning to do what makes me happy, without guilt or explanation. I was unlearning behaviors that hadn't suited me or served me. I was learning to accept that it was ok to make decisions that would bring me happiness and joy. Painting brought me joy and made me happy.

So, I had an idea that I wanted to incorporate into this revisited passion of mine. In the room that essentially became my painting studio, I asked Momma and Ava to assist me in creating a mural on the wall to serve as a constant reminder to always put myself first. Ava shouted, "Um I'll sit on the sideline and observe 'cause bitch I'm not messing up this French manicure." Momma held up her glass of champagne and shook her head in agreement with Ava's comment then offered, "You are the painter my love. Do what makes you feel good. We'll stand by and watch the magic unfold." I laughed out loud at them because the champagne had definitely kicked in. Then I felt another wave of anxiousness come over me. This time it was obvious to Momma, and she walked over to me, placing her hand on my shoulder. She leaned into me and whispered, "It's ok to feel baby. Take this all in. You have been to hell and back. Literally. But my God is good, and he said not today, Satan! You are blessed and covered by his grace and mercy. Please allow yourself to feel that, Lena. You've been this way since you were a child; suppressing what you feel, suppressing what you want to say or express to accommodate other people. Stop that, today. As your mother, it's one of the hardest things to observe especially when I see how it's tearing you apart and breaking you down." I was sobbing now and replaying in my head everything I had gone through over the last several years. These had been painful and tragic and gruesome and sickening experiences. I felt myself losing my balance when Ava walked over and placed her arm around my waist to steady me. Momma continued in a louder, firmer tone, "But you are now in the season of healing baby. Healing for your mind, healing for your spirit, healing for your body, and healing for your soul. You will have moments of feeling great and equally have moments when you are at your lowest low. That's all part of the healing journey. You have been through a physically and mentally traumatic experience baby at the hands of someone you loved. It's okay to accept that. But it's not your responsibility to understand it. You may never understand it. He hurt you in the literal and figurative sense and it cannot be forgotten or undone and no one can rebound from something like that overnight. No one. I don't give a damn how many doctors you see, how quickly the scabs or scars heal and even disappear. The pain is still there and only God and his timing will bring you through to the other side. Only God will give you the strength to come through this, to see brighter days, and even forgive. You hear me? So, take it all in, acknowledge it, embrace it, feel it, and keep moving forward. You may not be fully healed yet. But you are finally free." We stood there together, crying, and embracing. Then in her typical fashion Ava took a swig of her champagne and chimed in to say, "Shit, I don't know why the hell you been paying for therapy all this time. Momma just got you smooth together in 15 minutes. For free." We burst out into raucous laughter and sat on that patio for hours. This is what I missed and what meant the world to me. Regardless of the tears, I hadn't felt this good overall in years.

Eighteen: **Focus**

~ the center of interest or activity ~

-18-

My final occupational therapy appointment resulted in good news; I was officially done! I had made tremendous progress and was told that I could be the *poster child* of what dedication and fortitude looked like. Hell, it wasn't hard for me to be diligent and would have been easier to fall into a "pity party" mode but I didn't have time for that shit. I was like "Come on let's go, let's get this party started." I wanted to do what I needed to get back to my sense of self. And I was tired of having these folks come to my house and equally tired of going to outpatient therapy. So, I was fully invested in the therapeutic activities from the beginning and fortunate to have some great people to work with. You know there's a lot of vulnerability and patience required when you're at the mercy of others. And my track record as a patient was less than stellar. In fact, I'd been called a bitch by a doctor or nurse on more than one occasion. But when I set my mind to something I am all in. That's not to say that I didn't struggle at times because there were some grueling days for sure. The injuries to my ankle and wrist were pretty significant and you don't realize how dependent you are on your limbs until you don't have full mobility. I have a whole new respect for occupational therapists, especially mine. I got exactly what I asked for when I said "Let's get this party started" because these motherfuckers worked me to tears at every session. And despite every name I threw at them ("asshole", "bitch ass", "fucker", "hoe") or the meaner things I'd say like ("I hate you", "yo momma", "fuck you", "kiss my ass", "you do this shit bitch", "get the hell away from me") they stood by my side without failure or hesitation. It takes a truly committed professional to withstand what I threw at them. But they hung in there with me, so I did my part in tandem. I can say, however, that of all the harsh and terse language I'd used I never once said, "I quit." I never missed an appointment, and I was never late. I was committed to my physical healing and rejuvenation. Rainey, my therapist who assisted me with regaining full mobility with the wrist, was a living example of an angel. She always had a smile on her face, and she always thanked me for showing up. I could never understand that. Like, why are you thanking me? I'd ask myself, especially after how I would behave at times. But over time, she taught me that it was easier for her to acknowledge that while the patient needed her to aid in their healing, they were not obligated to continue to see her. So, when they showed up, she thanked them, because it was another opportunity for her to do what she loved. She loved what she did and did what she loved. And she was excellent at it. When our final session ended, I cried like a baby because she had made an indelible impact on me. It was about far more than the steps toward improving mobility, she taught me about patience gentleness, and even forgiveness. She would say, "It's easy to walk in here and be angry. Be angry at your circumstances, at the injury, and the people involved in getting you here. But the healing and the work you put in isn't about anyone but you. Why be angry at the things you have no control over and cannot change? Focus on what you can do now because it will benefit you in the end." The most significant aspect of my experience with Rainey was she was the one who essentially helped me regain the use of the wrist. This was the wrist I used to paint with. In the beginning, I was so mean and cold towards her. She could have easily asked to be replaced, but she did not. She did not give up on me. Instead, she would ask questions from the moment she started our sessions. "Tell me about yourself, Ms. Lena. Where did you grow up? What is your favorite show on TV right now? What did you eat today? What's your favorite color? Are you happy? What motivates you? When did you start painting?" In reflection, I recognize this was part of the therapeutic practice. Ask questions to the patient as a method of distraction. By keeping me talking about myself, it was easier for her to apply pressure, twist to the left, pull to the right, etc. She would rather I be annoyed by her questions than her therapeutic technique. And it worked. Before long, she didn't have to ask questions. We talked about everything. Soon I began asking questions and, while it is not common for this to happen, she felt comfortable responding to me and sharing things that I'm certain she didn't typically share with others. We eventually talked about everything. Rainey opened up once and told me that she had been in an abusive relationship with someone she thought was her "forever" partner. Her guy was well-educated, handsome, financially stable and came from a good family. They'd had a whirlwind courtship and knew right away that they wanted to be together. She said they quickly became engaged and soon thereafter married in a *fairytale* ceremony. They spent their honeymoon in Turks & Caicos and soon after returning she found out she was pregnant. She came up with a sweet way to share the pregnancy news with her husband. Their families planned to come together to view their wedding photos so she planned to tell everyone at the same time. Rainey said the evening had gone well and everyone was thrilled to see the wedding photos. They had even watched the videos laughing at random guests and their antics. She said she stood up and said, "Well everyone, Adam and I first want to thank you all for being here today to share in this wonderful journey with us. We are so happy and look forward to spending the rest of our lives together." She said Adam smiled at her and grabbed her tight around the waist. "Yes, we couldn't be any happier, truly." Rainey cleared her throat and said, "Well honey, on that note I have something else to say…we're pregnant!" Their parents collectively yelped with joy. "No way! Oh, my goodness! This is amazing news! You two didn't waste any time!" Rainey said she was smiling so hard her cheeks hurt. Then she noticed that Adam had released his arm from her waist. She turned to him to lean in for a kiss and he retreated. She said no one noticed because they were too busy shrieking about the baby news. But she noticed. He became cold and distant from that moment. They had discussed waiting to have kids but she had no idea he'd have this reaction. That was the beginning of what became a tumultuous 5 years between them. As time passed, he was verbally and emotionally abusive to her and their daughter. But what brought their relationship to a complete halt was when he struck her in front of their daughter. She replayed the moment for me, and it immediately brought tears to her eyes. "I had taken a lot from him. And for all things considered, I should have left him much sooner than I did. But I stayed. And I put up with it." She wiped her tears away and smiled as she always did. "But the moment I saw him hold no regard for Taryn or the impact his behavior would have on her, I knew that was enough. She deserved better. I deserved better. So, I left that day. With no hesitation and no regret." I sat in silence taking in everything she had so freely shared with me and reflecting on my own experiences as a child. What would have happened in my life if Momma had taken that same approach and stuck to it? How differently would that decision have shaped me and my life choices? Rainey went on, "I had to put my feelings aside for the sake of my child. I needed to choose what was best for her. Everything I did beyond that was centered around our needs, on our happiness. Adam has, in recent months, begun to show up for Taryn; probably more than he had ever done. I'm grateful for that because it will matter to her in the long run. But it's more important for me to show her that I am strong and happy and free to make choices that maintain those feelings. No one should be allowed or empowered to take that away." Rainey's words permeated my soul. They were simple but filled with conviction. Rainey was the epitome of what it meant to focus with intention. This is how I needed to move forward, with intention. Doing what I needed to find my happiness again in life. Now it was time for me to reset, refocus, and restart my life. I had an uphill battle of healing and recovery ahead of me, but I was ready.

Nineteen: **Forgive**

~stop feeling angry or resentful toward someone for (an offense, flaw, or mistake)

~

-19-

"Lena, you will never believe who I saw today!" Ava was screaming into the phone. I was almost afraid to ask but I reluctantly said, "Girl who and why are you screaming? Damn." She paused, took a deep breath, and said, "Mrs. Tiffany "Bitch Ass" Walters." I froze and almost dropped the phone. I hadn't heard that name in years. I hadn't thought about this person in years and prayed I'd never encounter any one of the Walters again for as long as I lived. But that wasn't reality and highly unlikely since I was in Chicago. I guess I had been fortunate to not have had a run-in up to this point. But of all people to see any of them, it shouldn't have been Ava. I felt sorry for Ms. Tiffany (*well not really*) because Ava likely went crazy on her ass. "Lena! Did you hear me?!" Of course, I had. I just couldn't find the words. But I choked back the vomit that was slowly rising in my throat and replied. "Did she see you? Where were you?" Ava was going a mile a minute. "Girl! I was walking into The Water Tower and heard someone call my name. I turned around and saw her walking towards me. I was like *I know this ain't the fuck who I think it is*. And she walked right up to me, smiling and shit. I was like *Is this shit really happening.* Then she said in that bougie-ass tone, 'O*h my goodness it's been so long but I knew it had to be you, you were always so beautiful.*' Lena girl, I just stood there. She was talking for forever but I don't think I heard most of what she was saying because I was in shock. Then I heard her say your name and I quickly came back to myself." There was a long pause and I finally said, "What did she have to say about me?" Ava responded, "Get this. She first asked if I still spoke with or was still in contact with you. Then she asked me how you were doing. She said she'd wanted to reach out to you or your parents many times over the last many years but wasn't sure how it would be received." I felt tears well up in my eyes and I felt anxiety sweeping over me in tandem. *Breathe in, breathe out, Breathe in, Breathe out*. "Reach out to me for what?! What in the fuck did she think she could say that I or my parents would want to hear?" Granted it had been years since college and my relationship with Ty but the mention of anything associated with that family, or that time in my life brought so many feelings to the surface that made me ill. Ava ranted about it for another 10-15 minutes and I finally asked how she ended the conversation. "Girl I just said, Lena is doing great." Knowing Ava the way I do, that's exactly what she said too, and then she probably stood there looking Mrs. Walters square in the eye. Ava chimed in, "Girl you know me. I stood right there looking that bitch dead in her motherfucking eyes. I was hoping she said something sideways 'cause I woulda beat her bougie ass right there at 900 N Michigan Ave. I mean that, like what the fuck??? These people are fucking crazy and got a lot of damn nerve!" I took a deep breath and said, "Ava, it's all good boo. I gotta let that shit go. I'd be lying if I said I wasn't affected by this because I am. But this isn't healthy. I have to let this go. I have to forgive. I have to forgive them all. Ava snorted. Sheeeeiiiiiiiit, I don't! Fuck them, Lena! They don't get to just do all this bogus shit and then get excused." I interjected.

"Ava, the forgiveness is not for them. Hell, it's not even about them. This is for me and my peace of mind. For my healing. I have walked through my life hiding myself from others. It was inevitable that one of us would run into the other. Today it was you. Tomorrow it may be Momma, Dada, or Lenny. And me soon thereafter. I can't run from it. I can't run from my past, my life. It is what it is. But I can't let this shit define and cripple me. I just can't." I stopped, feeling the tears now that were running down my cheeks. Ava interjected, "Yeah yeah, I hear all that psycho-babble shit, Lena! These people fucked your life up. They did some grimy shit and I can't forgive that. I won't! You better than me sis." I shook my head as I wiped the tears away. "I hear you A, but I can't hold onto that any longer. No one knows better than me what they did to me. I lived it. And what I realize now is that I've put forth more effort and energy managing everyone else's feelings and reactions about what happened to *ME*. I won't do that anymore either. I can't spend my time talking you off the ledge because you're beside yourself with anger about something that happened to me. Yes, what the Walters family did to me was fucked up and horrible, but life has gone on. If I make the choice to move on and not dwell on it, that's on me. It takes more for me to be angry and vengeful than to move on and forgive. And as difficult as that may seem to you, I would just ask that you respect my position." Ava began to cry but I kept speaking. "Now please don't misunderstand, I'm not looking for or expecting a conversation or phone call from Mrs. Walters or Ty but I'm also not going to stress myself out if something like that occurred. I get to choose how to respond to it if it ever came to that. I am no longer giving anyone that much power over me. I am learning every day how to regain my strength, my power, my peace. No one gets to take those things away from me ever again. No one. Ava Nichelle Martenson I love everything about you. You are my best friend. My sister. My confidante. My fiercest protector. But I need you to respect and do your best to understand where I am right now. And I certainly don't want you to have such a visceral reaction to something that no longer holds the weight on me that it once did. Bitch don't be getting arrested!" We both cracked up. "I mean it. I'm letting this shit go baby. I have to. We have to. Yo' ass might take a little longer to fully shake it off and I get that, but work on it, ok? For me?" Ava snorted. Then she said, "I got you til the world blow up bitch." I laughed. That I knew for sure.

In my next therapy session, I mentioned the encounter Ava shared and found myself going back to the beginning of it all. I was honest about my feelings and told my therapist how I felt the anxiety coming over and how I felt physically ill and found it hard to speak. She probed deeper asking very direct questions about why I thought I'd had such a major reaction. I told her I assumed it was because I hadn't fully recovered from the trauma and in reality, I never got to officially close that chapter of my life fully. Perhaps, I needed that closure. Then we spent time discussing aspects of the situation. I immediately went into a rant about being open and honest with Ty, recalling Ty's and my first meeting and deep, intimate connection. I tried to identify when or where things seemingly went off the rails. My therapist let me go on and on until I realized that I was babbling and making excuses. Then she reminded me that most of what I'd shared didn't matter because the situation still happened. It's not that she dismissed the experience, but she asked what I might have done differently if I had the option, and I couldn't respond to that. I honestly do not know what I would have done differently. And what did it matter now? That was the point she wanted to emphasize. The choices *then* don't have to be the same choices *now*. Every past choice informs a future choice. That's the takeaway, that's the lesson. Don't focus on what you can't change or control and live in the world of the *could've, would've, or should've.* Instead, just be present. Focus on what you can do today and, even with that, allow yourself grace to make poor decisions and choices, learn from them, and most importantly, forgive yourself. Forgiveness isn't about accepting and excusing other people's bullshit and bad behavior. But it is about not letting those things impact who you are and aspire to be. I am learning how to do that more and more with each day, but it is a process that takes having the love and support of a good solid network. I'm blessed to have that in my life. While my team may be small, it is mighty.

Twenty: **Fate**

~be destined to happen, turn out, or act in a particular way~

-20-

"Dr. Timmons, your 11 a.m. is here", I heard my new office administrator, Layna, say over the speakerphone. "Thanks, show her in please," I responded. A tall, thin young girl appeared in the doorway, and I stood up to welcome her to have a seat on the sofa. Her name was Monica, and she was 12 years old. In some ways, she reminded me of myself at that age. She was visibly shy and a bit awkward. There was a strong presence about her based on her height, but she was not certain of it or comfortable with it. "Welcome Monica. Please make yourself comfortable. Can I get you water, soda, or tea?" Monica smiled, shaking her head no. She was clearly nervous as she barely made eye contact with me. I reassured her this was a safe space, and that we would just take time today to get to know each other. I followed up by saying we could talk as much or as little as she wanted to. She smiled and then looked at me. I smiled back.

The session with Monica went well. It was the first week of seeing patients in over a year but it felt good and I seemed to get back into my "flow." My new office space was beautiful, and Layna was an amazing addition to the practice. I had hoped to be able to coax Nadia into coming to work for me in the new space but being in the suburbs was too far of a commute for her. I understood that, but it sucked, I missed having her with me. She knew me and I trusted her tremendously. Nadia had always supported me and been privy to the aspects of my past that most would have run away from. I will never forget how she helped to console me that day when Erica showed up at my office. She could have left and never come back after all of that. But she stood by me and never thought less of or judged me. For that, I will be eternally grateful, and she will always have a place within my professional practice and in my life. Layna was, however, adapting very nicely. She is bubbly, in a refreshing sort of way which I appreciate especially when the days are long and mentally heavy. She is organized and very systematic in her style of managing the office and my patient calendars, which is necessary and welcomed. She came as a referral from Nadia so I didn't hesitate to meet with her and soon came to feel certain about moving forward. I must admit, I was nervous about bringing her on because for a moment I'd wondered what Nadia may have shared with her. Had she mentioned anything about the things that took place? In my gut I knew better than that, Nadia was not only a professional, but she had never, ever given me reason to feel that I couldn't trust her sense of loyalty. She was a vault. I was tripping. And so, Layna was now my "*rider*" for all that meant. We would be in the trenches together and I needed to know that she could be trusted, relied upon and most importantly, that she could and would hold anything she came to know or experience in the strictest of confidence. There could be no deviations from that.

The months that followed were moving along very fast and my practice was getting a lot of traction. I had rebuilt my client base and the referrals were booming. Soon

I was so booked out, it was hard for anyone "new" to get on my calendar. I brought on another junior office administrator to assist Layna because she was swamped and working overtime to keep things in order. We spent a lot of time together after hours; I was writing up patient notes and she was organizing files online as well as managing physical files which were also maintained onsite. We agreed that these longs days and nights were a lot to handle for the two of us. After several weeks of interviewing, I came across the profile of a college student named Ariane. She was 20 years old, in her senior year at Loyola Chicago *which is my alma mater* and pursuing a degree in Clinical Psychology. Of course, these factors were of great interest to me and piqued my desire to learn more about her. She was able to clearly articulate her goals to me and shared how she felt working in a setting like this with my guidance would further her passion about the field. I was never more impressed and intrigued by someone this young. She knew what she wanted and stood firm in her plans on how to achieve it. Ariane came from a single-parent home and worked extremely hard to progress towards her aspirations. Her mother passed away when she was 2 years old, and she had been raised by her father. She was his only child. Ariane was so poised, and polite. She spoke with such conviction during our interview even in the face of uncertainty. But for the things she was certain of, you were assured that she knew and meant exactly what she stated. For some strange reason, there was something about her and her energy that moved me deep inside. I felt an odd sense of connection to her. I wanted her around me so that I could offer more and pour into her. She shared countless stories with me and Layna about her childhood that were so personal and intimate. One story she shared was about her having to call her Dad to tell him she'd started her period at school. She said, "I was like, Daddy I need you. Something happened and it involves blood." And hung up the phone. Layna and I were cracking up because we could only imagine what her Dad must've been thinking. Ariane said her Dad frantically rushed into the school's office asking for her and if she was ok. When the school nurse greeted him she chuckled. “Yes, Mr. Wilkerson, Ari is fine. She started her menstrual cycle. Can you please step back here with me, and I’ll bring her to you? I’m sorry she scared you.” Ari said all the women in the office were giggling and eyeing her Dad at the same time. He was a very handsome guy. And most people knew that he was single and solely focused on raising Ariane. To hear about a man raising his daughter alone literally moved me to tears so I can imagine how they must have felt in that moment, which is such a special time typically shared between a mother and daughter. Ariane laughed as she told the story, “He was so frustrated but relieved that day. I cannot begin to know what he must have been thinking as he rushed to get to me but in retrospect, I probably could have given him more information to go on before I hung up on him.” She smiled big and shook her head clearly lost in that memory for a second. She continued, “Daddy has always taken things in stride. I wasn’t a problematic child by any means, but there were gaps in the ways that we could connect because, you know, he's a man. At times, I've overshared and at other times I'd have to *dumb it down* so as not to make him uncomfortable. I don't come from a big family at all, so I didn't have a ton of females to lean into. It was just my grandmother on Daddy's side. My maternal grandmother died when I was 6 and my aunt, my Mom's sister, wasn't consistent. Daddy said she struggled with my mother's passing and while she had children as well, I never really spent time with them. So, it was just me and Daddy." She sat still and quiet, again seemingly lost in the moment of sharing and reminiscing. She was put together, clean, and polished. All the things. But there was a brokenness about her that I could relate to. I wanted to know more, to fully understand her, and in some way give her back some of the pieces that were missing from her life. She felt comfortable with me (and Layna), so I wanted to nurture our connection and growing bond.

My therapy sessions had intensified over the course of the next many months with more and more revelations about my life; past and present. I'd shared that I'd formed this amazing relationship with these two ladies in my practice and it was refreshing for me. I'd unofficially become a mentor and inspiration to them that not only fed their souls but also my own. It became a reflective experience for me because I could recognize my own insecurities, feelings of ineptitude and overall fear which informed my life's choices. While my upbringing was not horrible by any stretch of the imagination there were deeps gaps and deeper wounds that contributed to the ways I showed up and presented myself. I could never be as open and honest as Ariane was at the age of 20. I was always so unsure of myself for as far back as I could recall but I learned to dress it up, mask it and play the role. It was an act that I perfected to be able to move ahead, achieve the goal, perform, and deliver. I was not and had not been living in my authenticity. Therapy offered the framework and tools to now begin to step into the skin I'm in and accept it, flaws and all. This was some scary shit because I have no clue who the fuck I really am. I'd listen to Ariane speak so impactfully about how her Dad allowed her to be exactly who she was without trying to fit into a mold that suited his needs or the perceptions of others. This was so unlike what I'd been taught, how I'd been raised. Good looks and looking the part was our family mantra. "Yeah right!" I recalled saying in one of my sessions. "Look where that shit got me!" I'm 40ish trying to figure myself out. I've lived a lifetime of experiences that most would never have survived. I guess there is something positive to be said about that. I am nothing if not resilient. But Ariane's confidence seemed to give me fuel to want to do the work on myself and learn to love my life again.

One busy afternoon, a month or so prior to hiring Ariane, I was sitting in my office going through mail when Layna popped her head in. "Dr. Timmons, you have a call on line 3". I looked up, "Oh thanks Layna. Is my next appointment here yet? If so, I'll take this call and then let you know when I'm ready." I looked up at the clock, it was 3:45p and my next appointment was at 4p. Layna answered,

"Yes, he's here. Just let me know when you're ready." I took a quick swig of water and picked up line 3. "Good afternoon, this is Dr. Timmons." A man on the other end responded, "Dr. Timmons, this is Charles Arthington with Arthington, Joneson and Smith, LLC. We are the firm representing Troy Bowers in the criminal sexual assault case." I froze. *Breathe in, Breathe out.* He continued, "I am calling to inform you that our client has plead guilty to the charges of aggravated domestic battery, sexual assault, leaving the scene of the crime and tampering with evidence. The case will not go to trial as we originally discussed with your attorney. You may have already been told this information, as I would assume your attorney already informed you, but I wanted to personally reach out to you to let you know about this new revelation. Mr. Bowers is being held but will likely be released on bond pending final sentencing." I took a deep breath and responded, "Thank you for contacting me, I'll reach out to my attorney." I hung up. I found my hands shaking and my palms were sweating. I took another deep breath and finished the glass of water in front of me. It was 3:55p and almost time for my next appointment so I had to pull myself together. I got through the session without a hitch and escorted the young man I'd just seen out to his mother who was waiting in the lobby. I asked Layna to schedule the next appointment and darted back into my office. Immediately I contacted my attorney. He apologized to me for having to sit through that conversation which of course triggered the hell out of me. He was pissed that the other firm even had the audacity to contact me directly. But told me it was a scare tactic to see if I would retract anything that I'd stated when we initially filed the case against Troy. In the state of Illinois, it was not uncommon for people in a domestic battery claim to change their story which then dismisses the case against the assailant. I was absolutely not going to be that person today or ever. In fact, I was proud of my ability to push through the entire call. Therapy played a huge role in that. The *Lena of old* would have fallen apart and passed out or thrown up;

or all the above. My attorney told me he'd get back to me once he'd contacted the other firm and let me know the latest. He assured me, nonetheless, that Troy would no longer be of any consequence in my life. I had put so much time and energy into pressing charges, having to relive and recount the horrific events of that day with police and attorneys that I would not give in because of this one stupid ass and insensitive phone call. Fuck that. He did it. He has to pay for it. And life goes on. I have so much to look forward to.

There were other positive things happening around me and within my family dynamic. A true testament to what faith, hard work and commitment look like. Momma and Dada found their way back together and were stronger than ever before. I don't know that I'd ever seen them be so openly affectionate and attuned to each other. It looked good on them. They took steps on their own to seek counsel through their pastor. I was shocked. I knew Momma would often speak with the pastor, but Dada was so hung up on his image that I couldn't believe he would allow himself to be so open, so vulnerable. I guess the thought of actually losing Momma shook him up and shifted his mindset. Dada shared with me that he realized a lot of his issues stemmed from his relationship with my Ganna and his upbringing. There was so much to unpack there and I asked him if he would want to go deeper into it to fully understand it all. He said he was not ready but maybe in time. Regardless, I was proud of him. Proud of both of them. It gave me hope that one day I would find a partner who would commit themselves to the relationship and to doing whatever it takes to be together.

Lenny was also in therapy and working hard on his anger issues. After the horrific situation between me and Troy, he spiraled and we ended up having an intervention with him. He was fixated on finding Troy and making him pay for the pain and trauma he had inflicted on me. Unfortunately, his obsession was affecting his relationship with us, he was placed on leave from work and sunk into a depression. I had to have a "come to Jesus" conversation with him and say, 'You can't be more fixed on revenge than me! Let this shit go, brother, please. This is vengeance killing you. Life can be fucked up Lenny. Things come apart, but they can also come back together again. You have to know that, and you have to believe that. Please stop this. Now." After that hard conversation, Lenny went right into therapy. He knew he needed help and also recognized that he was using my situation as some sick validation for his unacceptable behavior. It took a toll on the whole family. But I am so proud of him. He did the work on himself and now understands the impact it was having on him and his ability to cope. He learned this was an issue that stemmed from our childhood. Of course, it did. It all did. However, we've both learned that we do not have to stay stuck in those dark and scary places.

We do the work to be our best selves every day, always, and in all ways. Life presents opportunities for learning, lending, and leveling. I am a walking testament of each of those aspects presenting themselves along my journey. Even amongst the trials and tribulations that my story may have been riddled with, I'm still here. I am learning everything I can about myself good and bad; I'm lending my experiences and insights to those who are interested in them and I'm damn sure leveling up to always show up as the absolute best version of my true self every fucking day. Know that. I am Lena Joi Timmons; the story continues...

Outro

On the night of my 43rd birthday, Ava and I were out celebrating and having drinks. We were at one of my favorite places looking out at Lake Michigan and listening to good house music. I was feeling great and looking even better if I say so myself. I felt sexy and free. The weather that night was perfect, a combination of warmth and wind. But not too much. Just the slightest and softest breeze. The air even smelled good. All these beautiful people milling around, laughing, smiling, dancing and living in the moment. I had missed this feeling and I hadn't been this happy or content in years. As usual, my beautiful *sister girl* Ava was doing her thing, loudly and proudly. She was sipping champagne and *catcalling* from our table. "Hey now cuties!" She yelled over to a group of guys walking past us. They all laughed and smiled, pointing their fingers at her. I shook my head and took another sip of my champagne. "Wait, where y'all going? Come over here and say Happy Birthday to my sister!!", she hooted. They yelled back "Happy Birthday sister!!" We both cracked up laughing. This was everything.

It was just like back in the day. I closed my eyes to take it all in. Life felt good. Normal. We laughed and ate and drank even more and then the strangest thing happened. A barmaid walked over to our table with a glass of champagne and placed it in front of me. I looked puzzled and said, "I didn't order this." She grinned and replied, "I know. The guy sitting over there sent it. And he said Happy Birthday." She turned to walk away and Ava asked, "Wait, what guy? Where he at?" The lady pointed to a handsome man sitting, dressed in all white at a table with a few other people. He was looking and smiling directly at me. I smiled back. I felt hot all of a sudden. "Goddamn Lena, who is that?," Ava asked so loudly that I was sure the guy heard her. When he stood up, I was almost certain of it. He casually walked over to us. "Hello", he said with a deep, sultry voice. He had the whitest teeth I'd ever seen. We both giggled and said "*Hello*" in unison. "I sent the champagne over since it's your birthday. Happy Birthday, Miss Lena." He grabbed my hand and kissed it lightly. I was hot as hell and for a second, I thought I'd peed on myself because my panties got wet, instantly. Ava shrieked and said, "Aw shit! Damn!" I pulled my hand away slowly and asked, "Do we know each other?" He responded, "No. Well, yes. Indirectly. You know my daughter. Ariane. She mentioned to me earlier today that you were celebrating your birthday tonight and that this is your favorite spot. I'm here all the time, knew I'd be here tonight and hoped I'd finally get to meet you. I've heard nothing but amazing things about you. You've made and indelible impact on Ari. Ava leaned over and whispered, "Indelible impact… girl let him eat yo coochie!" She burst out laughing and I tried my best to hold it in. "Ah, you're Mr. Wilkerson. I'm so happy to meet you. Ari has told me so much about you." I was trying desperately to redirect the tone of the conversation because Ava's comment messed me up. This man was FOINE as hell. His smile was intoxicating, he smelled delicious, and he was tall. He had a beautiful smooth peanut butter complexion, and his lips were soft. I remembered that from the kiss on my hand. Ava saw someone she knew and said, "Nice to meet you…." Mr. Wilkerson replied, "Donovan, Van for short. Nice to meet you as well Miss Ava." Ava turned to me and said, "I'll leave you to it. I see Cam and Cindy over there. I'm gonna go over and say hi." She leaned in again like she was gonna kiss my cheek but instead she whispered slowly, "Let him eat yo coochie bitch, or I'll let him eat mine." I burst out laughing and pushed her away. "Bye Donovan! Van for short!" she said loudly as she sauntered off. Van asked, "May I sit?" I nodded and smiled, blushing again. We sat and talked for hours. In fact, we talked for so long, we shut the place down. Ava came back over, feeling no pain from all the cocktails she'd had and said she was ready to go. Neither of us drove so we were planning to share a cab ride home. Van interjected, "I'm happy to drop you off. Both of you." Ava smiled and I reached over to pinch her before she said anything crazy. "Oh, okay, are you sure?" He stood up and motioned for our waitress, "I'm certain." When the waitress reached our table, he handed her his credit card.

Ava looked at me and smiled again. "Well happy damn birthday, Lena Joi!" I looked up at Van and said, "I really appreciate this, thank you so much." He grabbed my hand and said, "It was my pleasure. Thanks for allowing me to share your special day. I enjoyed our time together this evening. I can only hope there is a chance to have more like this one." We walked to Van's car. He opened the doors for Ava and me. He dropped Ava off first and walked her to the door. She yelled to me, "Sis, I love you. Let me know when you make it home. Oh yeah, offer Van something to eat when you get there. I'm sure you can find something for him to eat!" I lowered my head and shook it vigorously. This crazy ass heffa, I thought to myself. Van got back to the car and asked if I needed anything before heading to my house. He said, "I hope you're ok with me taking you home. I didn't think about that before offering and assuming you'd be ok with it. I just couldn't allow you and Ava to take a cab, while I'm there with my vehicle. My Daddy taught me to be a gentleman always so it's just what I know to do." I paused.

I was taking all this in. It had been a very long time since I'd been near a man or even thought a man. I wasn't certain I'd ever have the desire to be with anyone or entertain a man's company ever again. But this felt nice. It felt organic though we did have a connection through Ariane. I told him I was fine with him taking me and that I truly appreciated him for it. When we pulled into the driveway Van said, "I guess we're here. He got out and walked over to my door, opened it, and held out his hand. I grabbed it and stepped out of the car. He walked me to the door and we stood there, awkwardly. Well, Miss Lena. Here we are. Thanks again for allowing me to spend time with you on your birthday. I had an amazing time." He grabbed my hand again and kissed it lightly. Yup, I was wetter than before. This time I let him hold it a bit longer before finally pulling it away. "I thank you. Van. You have no idea how much I needed this. Best birthday I've celebrated in a very long time." Then unexpectedly, I leaned in and kissed him slightly on the lips. When I pulled back he said, "Aw man, I'd better walk away now before I can't. Can I call you? Please say yes." I asked for his phone. I put my number in it and added my name, Lena Joi. He looked down at it, smiled and rubbed his hand slightly along the side of my cheek. He turned to walk away and said, "Looking forward to it. I promise." I giggled and asked, "Looking forward to what exactly?" He yelled out, "Bringing you joy. You deserve it." I blushed, walked inside, and closed the door.

Before I could set my purse down, Ava was already calling. I answered and before I could say anything beyond *hello* all I heard was, "Biiiiiiiiiittttccccccchhhhhhhhh…" We giggled. I don't know what will happen next with Van but right now it feels exciting and definitely has made me feel good. Ava and I cackled for another hour or so. She finally said, "Ok I'm tired. Going to bed. I love you bitch. Happy Birthday. Go change yo panties." I hung up and noticed I'd missed a text from Van. It read, "I hope I'm not out of line for this, but it took everything in me to keep from grabbing you at your door. I don't know what will happen next, Lena

Joi, but I want to figure some things out. I hope you let me. Goodnight. Speak soon." He hung up. I felt hot again. *Breathe in. Breathe out. Breathe in. Breathe out.* Lord help me. The way he says my name makes my liver quiver. I stood in the mirror and smiled at my reflection. Then in a soft, sultry tone I leaned in closer and said, "I'm looking forward to it too, Van." I was looking forward to many things. This was indeed a great way to start. Stay tuned.

About the Author

Photo collection by Sydney Payne Photography

Dr. Kijana (Kai) Jackson is native to Chicago, IL; born and raised on the south side of the city. She relocated to Houston, TX to be nearer to her three children, and two grandchildren. She holds a Ph.D. in Business Psychology. This is her first fiction-published work. Outside of writing, she is also a singer and songwriter.

In 2022, Dr. Jackson founded IntHERsections LLC, a non-profit organization. The mission of the organization stems from Dr. Jackson's deep-seated passion for advocating and supporting the health and wellness of young African American women. Offering guidance with their personal and professional goals, Dr. Jackson's philosophy centers on caring for the "whole woman"; mind, body, and soul. With mental health becoming increasingly important, her ultimate goal is to provide support from the inside out.

Made in the USA
Columbia, SC
29 March 2025

55793003R00172